Dear Reader,

Everyone here at Scholastic is shocked: The mystery of Ulysses Moore grows more and more complex every day. Our fearless editor, Michael Merryweather, has unearthed a second manuscript. We had no idea that he would find something so fascinating and important.

Here's a note that Michael sent us just after he found the second manuscript.

Thanks so much for taking this journey with us,

Your friends at
Scholastic

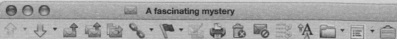

From: Michael Merryweather
Date: January 10, 2006 11:36 PM
To: Everyone at Scholastic
Subject: A fascinating mystery

To Everyone at Scholastic:
I am writing to you from my little room in Cornwall, England. I've found a second manuscript! This one is written in a code or some sort of ancient language, as well. I'm working hard to translate it. I just knew more of Ulysses's writing was out there. Julia, Jason, and Rick stumbled onto something very mysterious in the last book, and there are answers in this manuscript. Many of them. How did the kids get to Egypt? And what year is it?

I won't be able to sleep until I figure this out.

I'll send more information just as soon as I can.

Michael

ULYSSES MOORE

THE LONG-LOST MAP

APPLE SERIES

SCHOLASTIC INC.

New York Toronto London Auckland Sydney
Mexico City New Delhi Hong Kong Buenos Aires

ISBN-13: 978-0-439-77673-8
ISBN-10: 0-439-77673-2

Text by Pierodomenico Baccalario
Original title: *La Bottega delle Mappe Dimenticate*
Original cover and illustrations by Iacopo Bruno
Graphics by Iacopo Bruno and Laura Zuccotti
Translation by Leah Janeczko
Editorial project by Marcella Drago and Clare Stringe

Special thanks to James Preller
Design by Timothy Hall

12 11 10 9 8 7 6 5 4 3 2

Printed in the U.S.A.

First paperback printing, September 2007

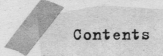

Contents

THE LONG-LOST MAP

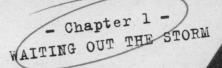

- Chapter 1 -
WAITING OUT THE STORM

First draft translation of Ulysses Moore's second notebook

I found this Polaroid that was taken in Egypt. It's very strange — I've done a lot of research, and buildings and statues like this no longer exist!

The light from the high tower of Argo Manor flickered and faded in the face of the storm. Like an exhausted boxer in the late rounds of a fight, it seemed to struggle against the night itself, weakening against the onslaught of wind and rain. A ferocious gale swayed the tall trees like blades of grass. *Crack, boom!* A massive limb shattered and fell to the ground. Far below, along the shoreline, armies of waves pounded against the rocks.

Inside the great house, Nestor checked and double-checked the windows and doors. He limped from room to room, finding his way through the darkness amid the ancient furnishings of the house. He knew Argo Manor by heart, as if he carried a secret map of the place, and easily navigated around stuffed chairs, desks, coffee tables, Egyptian statues, and relics from lost continents. He instinctively ducked his head before passing under the Venetian chandelier in the sitting room. After many years of loyal service, Nestor's knowledge of every dark corner of the house was nearly perfect.

Making his way past the staircase, Nestor reached the grand portico at the front of the house and paused before the large glass windows. Looking out at the lush, rain-drenched gardens, he leaned against the base of the statue of a woman mending a fishing net. Illuminated by eerie flashes of lightning through the windows, the fisherwoman almost looked alive.

Nestor rubbed his hands together briskly. He climbed the stairs, passing the long row of portraits of the house's former owners, and entered the tower room. He cast a reassuring glance at the diaries and the collection of model ships, and then returned to the ground floor. Everything was as it should be, each item in its place. A single diary was missing, of course, but Nestor took that as a good sign.

He came at last to the great stone room and flicked on a light. Scattered on the floor were pencils and sheets of paper, just where Jason, Julia, and Rick had left them after spending the afternoon solving the puzzle of the four locks.

Owl. Porcupine. Elephant. Newt.

And so it was, he noted. They had managed to unlock the door. . . .

Nestor gazed at the heavy door. Its ancient wood was scarred with burns and gashes. And now it was locked again. Sealed off once more. There was no getting in from this side. He knew that much. There was nothing to be done except wait.

"Let's hope they are safe," the caretaker whispered aloud, passing his hand across the wood of

the mysterious door. He glanced at his watch. The long, slender hands swept gracefully through time in a perfect circle. "They should be there by now," he figured. His teeth clenched anxiously.

"It has begun."

- Chapter 2 -
THE WALL

Behind the mysterious door, beyond the dark passages, Jason, Julia, and Rick suddenly stopped in their tracks.

The three friends had had an incredible adventure over the past twenty-four hours. Jason and Julia Covenant were eleven-year-old twins, and Rick Banner was their newest friend. The twins had just moved from London to Kilmore Cove, a sleepy little town along the coast of Cornwall. But there was nothing sleepy about what they'd discovered behind the unusual door in the oldest room of their new home, Argo Manor. Following clues that they suspected had been left by the house's previous owner, Ulysses Moore, the twins and Rick had succeeded in opening the door and revealing what lay behind it: a long stone passageway full of riddles and puzzles that the kids had managed to decipher one by one. And the passageway led to something beyond their wildest imaginations . . . the *Metis,* a great sailing ship anchored in an enormous grotto. That ship had carried them here — to ancient Egypt. Where now someone — or some*thing* — was banging on the other side of the wall.

The tapping was methodical, repeating over and over. One knock. Two knocks. One knock. Then two more in quick succession. They were light taps, almost as if someone was trying to send a message, but uncertain of how to do it, or to whom it was being sent.

"Why are they knocking?" Julia asked in a hushed voice.

"Someone must have heard us talking," Rick replied.

Jason put his ear against the bricks.

"What do you hear?" Julia asked.

"I only hear you, since you won't stop jabbering!" Jason replied. He rapped once, then twice against the wall.

Julia gave her twin brother an annoyed look. "So *now* what are you doing?"

Jason grinned. "I'm answering them."

Behind the twins, Rick Banner shook his head. "Maybe that's not such a hot idea. I don't think we should let anyone know we're here. . . ."

His words were cut off by the sound of two distinct raps, then a much louder one. Jason raised his eyebrows. He replied with a thundering smack against the wall.

"Jason!" Julia hissed. "Didn't you listen to what Rick just said?"

"*Shhh!* I hear something," Jason said, his ear pressed hard against the wall.

Then came a series of noises that were difficult to make out, followed by a moment of silence and, finally, a sharp, grating screech.

"Did you hear that?" Jason asked.

Julia rolled her eyes. "No, I missed it," she said. "It wasn't loud or annoying or anything — like fingernails against a chalkboard."

Jason ignored her sarcasm. "But what *was* it?"

"It sounded like metal," Rick said. "Metal scraping against stone."

They stood there, listening attentively, but the mysterious noises seemed to have stopped. Then, suddenly, a puff of dust came rolling in from underneath the wall.

In an instant, Jason realized what was happening. He jumped back from the wall and shouted to the others, "Move! RUN!"

There was a *boom*, followed by a series of crashing noises. A massive cloud of dust billowed up around them, clogging their lungs.

Julia started to run down the stairs they'd climbed just moments before, encircled by a cloud of dust. She didn't look back, but she could still hear Jason's screams from behind her. "Run! Run!"

She doubled her speed and raced around the corner. Jason and Rick were right on her tail. Then Julia heard the sound of bricks tumbling, falling, crashing to the ground. Rick cried, "Go, Julia! Go!"

Julia reached the door they had come through. She yanked it open and bolted to the other side.

She found herself running in total darkness, as if in a nightmare. She tripped and fell hard to the floor . . . onto a rug.

A rug?

Julia heard the massive door swing shut behind her with a loud *clack*. Rick's cries and her brother's voice were cut off instantly, as if she had crossed into a soundproof room. It was like Rick and Jason were just *gone*, like they had never even existed.

Julia sprang to her feet. Where was she?

Around her were a rug, a little table, an armoire pushed into a corner, a blue couch, and a few armchairs. Outside, rain pounded against the windowpanes and wind banged the shutters.

"Argo Manor?" she asked, to no one in particular.

A man's shadow loomed up next to her. Julia screamed.

Nestor reached out and held her by the arms. "Julia? Are you all right?"

Julia opened her mouth, but she found she was unable to answer. She stared at the door, absently brushing the white dust from her face. What had

happened? How could this be? She didn't understand.

"Where are the others?" Nestor asked.

Julia blinked, uncertain.

"Rick and Jason?" Nestor repeated, his voice sharp
with fear. "What happened to them?"

Julia shook her head. Behind her, the door was
shut. The four keyholes, arranged in the shape of a
diamond, seemed to peer back at her.

Rick wasn't there. Jason wasn't there. She was the
only one who had returned. Julia shook her head
again, uncomprehending.

"I don't know," she said. "I don't know where
they are."

- Chapter 3 -
THE NIGHT VISITORS

I found this beautiful perfume bottle... I think it might have belonged to Oblivia Newton!

NEFER
PARFUMS

A car passed through the empty streets of Kilmore Cove. It was long, sleek, and luxurious. Tinted windows hid its passengers from view. Though its silent windshield wipers worked flawlessly, the road was scarcely visible in the storm. The high beams from the headlights barely sliced through the darkness. As the vehicle crested a hill, a sudden light blasted through the front windshield, blinding the driver, who stomped on the brakes in panic.

From the backseat came a woman's angry complaint. She rattled off a series of insults, concluding with a final demand, "Don't ever do that again, you thickheaded mule."

"But the lighthouse," explained Manfred, the driver. "The beacon blinded me. I couldn't see."

The woman, Oblivia Newton, reponded with icy silence. She was about as sympathetic as a cobra. So Manfred bit his tongue, lowered his head dutifully, and pressed his foot down on the accelerator. He steered the car through narrow, twisting streets, deeper into the heart of town.

"This isn't the way," Oblivia growled from the backseat.

Manfred eyed her stonily in the rearview mirror. "Just a shortcut, Ms. Newton," he answered. He eased the car past the town center, a circular plaza that featured a large equestrian statue. "Almost there," he muttered.

He pulled the car to a stop outside a simple house. No lights shone from within. There was no movement behind the windows. He killed the headlights and quieted the engine.

"Finally," Oblivia said, her voice betraying an unusual eagerness. She doused herself with perfume and stepped out of the car without waiting for her servant to open the door for her. "Quickly, Manfred," she said. "Get the umbrella, you fool. Must I tell you everything?"

Manfred paused a beat. "You want me to come?"

"Have you forgotten your job, Manfred?" Oblivia retorted. "We have a mission, and I may need your muscle." She turned and headed toward the old house. Grimacing, Manfred followed her.

Miss Cleopatra Biggles had spent every one of her sixty-five years in Kilmore Cove. She was born there, raised there, and, she hoped, would one day die there. But in all those years, she had never before been awoken in the middle of the night by someone knocking loudly on her front door. She fumbled for

the cord to the lamp on her nightstand and gave it a tug.

"Who in heaven's name could that be, Mark Antony?" she asked one of the two plump cats who had been sleeping at the foot of her bed.

Mark Antony leaped onto the windowsill. He stared out the window, his back arched. The second cat continued to snooze as though nothing had happened.

"I'm sorry to disturb you, Caesar," Miss Biggles murmured. "But I believe there's someone at the door. I do hope everything's all right."

Miss Biggles rubbed her eyes and reached for the alarm clock on the nightstand. Squinting, she saw that it was past midnight.

"Who could it be at this late hour?" she asked her cats.

Neither offered a reply.

Yet whoever it was, they were knocking again, this time even more loudly.

"Oh dear, oh dear," said a flustered Miss Biggles. She stepped into her woolen slippers, which had been carefully set beneath her bed. Unfortunately, in doing so she accidentally stepped on the tail of a third cat, who scrambled to the top of the headboard with a sharp mew. "I'm so sorry, Marcus Aurelius!" Miss Biggles apologized.

Patting her hair with frail hands, Miss Biggles

carefully made her way down the wooden staircase to the ground floor. She made sure not to step on any other cats.

"Careful, my sweeties! Please let me through!" Miss Biggles called down. At the sound of her voice, twenty-two cats — all residents of the Biggles home — watched and wondered what the old woman was up to now.

Miss Biggles peered through the smoky glass panel of her front door. But it was very dark and rainy, and her eyes were not what they used to be. She could only make out the shadowy outline of a person in the night.

Before opening the door, Miss Biggles cautiously slid the safety chain into its holder. She pulled the door open a crack. "Why, Ms. Newton, it's you!" she exclaimed in surprise. "Is there trouble?"

"Please open the door, Miss Biggles," Oblivia Newton instructed, forcing a smile. "This weather is fit for neither man nor beast."

Flustered, Cleopatra Biggles fumbled with the chain and finally managed to open the door. Oblivia Newton's high heels clicked against the floor as she swept into the house. At the sight of her, most of Miss Biggles's cats scampered off to hide in the shadows of the sitting room.

"Ms. Newton, what on earth has brought you

here at this hour?" wondered Miss Biggles. "I wasn't expecting guests and — oh dear, oh dear." She had turned to shut the door when a meaty hand pushed it all the way open. A bolt of lightning illuminated the heavy features of Manfred, who stood in the doorway, soaked from head to foot.

Cleopatra Biggles clutched her bathrobe to her chest, frightened. She glanced at Ms. Newton. "Is this man with you? What is going on? Oh dear, oh heavens . . ."

Oblivia ignored the worried old woman. Instead, she walked boldly into the hallway that led from the sitting room to the kitchen. She paused in front of a door that presumably led to the cellar and began searching the wall with her fingers.

"I need light," Oblivia snapped. "Miss Biggles," she demanded sharply, "I must have more light."

Miss Cleopatra Biggles, however, was still in a state of dumbstruck shock. The large, unpleasant man had her thoroughly frightened. Recognizing this, Oblivia sweetened her tone. "You have nothing to fear," she told Miss Biggles. "This is my driver, Manfred. It is so awfully wet outside, you understand."

Cleopatra Biggles nodded, though she did not understand at all. She managed to make a feeble gesture to the sitting room. "Please, do come in, Mr. Manfred," she said haltingly.

Meanwhile, Oblivia made clicking noises with her tongue as she puzzled over the door in the wall. Miss Biggles watched as the younger woman slipped off her fur coat, dropping it to the floor. Miss Biggles could not help but marvel at Oblivia's considerable beauty — as well as her odd choice of clothing. Oblivia Newton wore tall sandals that were laced halfway up her calves, a white loose-fitting skirt fastened around her waist with a belt of cords, and a ruffled top with leopard-spotted cuffs. Her long neck was adorned with a splendid gold necklace.

Miss Biggles smoothed back her hair and tugged at her thin, flowered nightgown. "Ms. Newton, have you been to a costume party?" the old woman wondered.

"Light!" Oblivia Newton demanded. "Turn on the light, Miss Biggles! And please keep your prattling to yourself."

Cleopatra Biggles found a wall switch and turned on the overhead lamp. She felt a wave of dread come over her. Something was terribly wrong. *Please*, she thought, *let no harm come to my dear cats.*

"At last!" exclaimed Oblivia. She seemed focused on a mark on the cellar door. "I believe we're in luck."

Miss Biggles held Mark Antony in her arms and stroked the cat nervously. "I-I don't understand," she stammered. "This is all very strange, Oblivia. It's the middle of the night and I really must insist . . ."

Oblivia slid her fingers over the lock of the old door. She bent to the floor and picked up a few grains of sand.

"As I said," Miss Biggles began again, now deeply worried, "I must protest. You simply cannot barge into my home and . . ."

"Manfred," spoke Oblivia, "I believe it's time for our kind host to take a nap."

At these words, Manfred's hand shot out and covered the old woman's mouth with a handker-chief soaked with chloroform. The old woman's eyes bulged open in fright, but in seconds they shut again. She slipped out of Manfred's thick arms and onto the floor, while her agitated cats skittered around her nervously.

"Sleep deep, you old crow," snarled Oblivia. Then to Manfred she said, "Put her on the couch, you lug. Do I have to explain everything to you? Can't you figure out the simplest things for yourself?"

"Sorry, Ms. Newton," he mumbled. "I'll try to do better."

Oblivia flashed an insincere smile. "Yes, do that," she said sarcastically. "And perhaps if you try very hard, you'll come up with an idea all by yourself. Wouldn't that be special?"

Manfred nodded, the words stinging his ears. He

wasn't dumb. He had a brain. He could do things. He had ideas of his own, plenty of them.

From inside her shirt pocket, Oblivia took out an old key with a cat-shaped handle. She slid it into the lock of the cellar door and turned the key.

Clack went the lock.

"I will see you later," she told Manfred. Glancing toward the sleeping body of Miss Biggles, Oblivia added, "Meanwhile, make yourself useful."

And with that, she opened the door.

But it did not lead to the cellar.

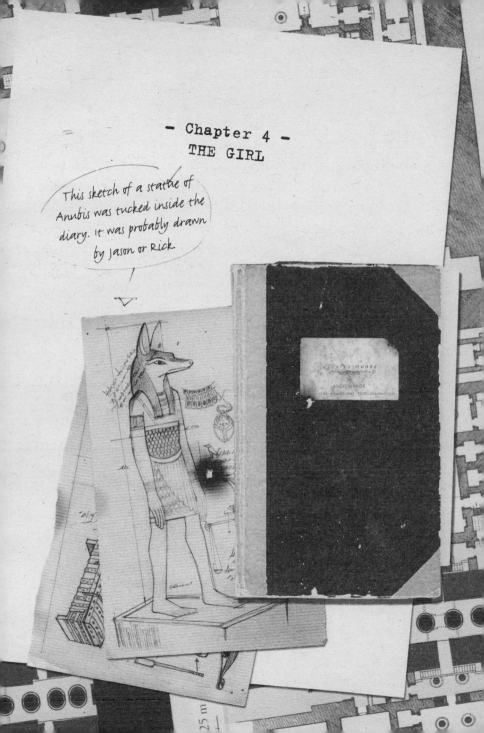

— Chapter 4 —
THE GIRL

This sketch of a statue of Anubis was tucked inside the diary. It was probably drawn by Jason or Rick

As the dust began to settle, the first thing Jason saw was the threatening face of a dog snarling through the pile of fallen bricks.

After a startled moment, Jason realized that it was only a stone statue. He recognized the dog from his history textbook. It was Anubis, the jackal-headed god of ancient Egypt. The god of the dead, to be exact.

It appeared that the heavy statue had been used to knock a hole through the wall.

Jason looked around, trying to get his bearings. Clouds of thick dust still hung in the air. "Julia?" he called, pulling himself to his feet. "Rick?"

Rick Banner was sprawled out a short distance from Jason. He had fallen at the bottom of the stairs.

"Are you okay?" Jason asked, hurrying to his friend.

"Yeah, I think so," Rick replied. "You?"

"I'm fine," Jason answered. "Where's my sister?"

"I have no idea," Rick answered, coughing from the dust. "She was right in front of me. I think she reached the door. She might be back in the grotto. Hold on, I'll go check."

"Wait!" Jason whispered a warning. He held up a hand and listened carefully, his head cocked to the side. He heard a voice moaning. It was coming from the other side of the wall. "Somebody's here," he said.

The two friends cautiously approached the statue of the god of the dead. They peeked through the hole in the wall. On the other side, buried beneath a large pile of rubble, was a girl. But it wasn't Julia.

"Help," the girl groaned.

Without hesitation, Jason and Rick climbed through the wall and pulled the girl out from underneath large shards of pottery. She looked dazed and disoriented. Somehow a large rack of clay pots had fallen on her. The girl appeared to be about their age. She was dressed in a dusty tunic, and her head was completely shaved with the exception of a long black braid on the side that hung down her back.

With Rick and Jason's help, the girl rose unsteadily to her feet. "Are you all right?" Jason asked. "You could have been killed."

The girl shook her head. "I'm not hurt," she said. "Just a bit of a headache. But look — I've made a terrible mess of things!" She rubbed her forehead and wiped both hands across the fine, porcelain features of her face.

Jason and Rick stared in disbelief at their surroundings. It was a room full of strangely crafted furniture — a massive foot carved in stone, crocodile-

shaped trunks, tables with legs that looked like bird claws, and countless broken pieces of clay jars that lay scattered around on the floor.

"You saved me," the girl finally said. "I owe you a debt of gratitude. If you hadn't pulled me out from under there, I might have suffocated."

Rick and Jason glanced at each other, not sure how to respond. "It was nothing," Rick finally said. "You don't owe us anything."

"No, I do," the girl answered. She suddenly seemed to remember the wall. She squinted to get a better look at the gaping hole.

She's nearsighted, Rick observed.

"Did you come from . . . the other side?" the girl asked, searching the faces of the two boys.

"Yes," Jason replied. "We were on the other side of the wall."

"Tell me," she said. "What is it like . . . on the other side?"

Jason and Rick exchanged a look. They seemed to reach a silent understanding. "Oh, there's nothing — nothing at all." Rick said at last. "Just the same things that are here. And, well, a lot of dust!"

"If my father finds out that I've caused this disaster," the girl said, "he'll be furious." She leaned against the statue of Anubis and asked, "That was you, wasn't it? I heard your voices. I banged on the wall . . . and you answered."

"I'm surprised you could hear us," Rick commented.

"Oh, I heard you easily!" the girl exclaimed. "That wall is as thin as a *seba*."

Rick stiffened. A *seba*? He quietly thumbed through the *Dictionary of Forgotten Languages.* There it was, a *seba*. He whispered to Jason, "A *seba* is a kind of umbrella. It's a word used in ancient Egypt."

A chill ran down Jason's spine. So it was true. But then how could they understand the language of this girl so easily? It wasn't possible. But yet . . . yet . . . here they were. Somehow they understood her, and she understood them.

Powerful magic, Jason concluded.

"I was searching for an *ostrakon*," the girl explained, "when I heard your voices."

"*Ostrakon*. A fragment of broken pottery used to write down brief sayings or curses," Rick whispered into Jason's ear.

The girl wasn't too bad-looking when you got used to her bald head. She continued with her explanation. "I walked up to the wall and knocked. Until you answered back, I feared that I had been imagining things. That's when I grabbed the statue of Anubis — I

used it to break down the wall to figure out what — or who — was on the other side. But as you can see," she said, gesturing to the rubble on the floor, "I am as clumsy as an ox. I must have accidentally bumped the pottery rack and made it fall on top of me."

Jason smiled. There was something about this girl that he liked.

"I am too curious," the girl suddenly scolded herself. "Father always says it, and he is right. I am always making a mess of things!"

She looked Jason in the eye. "I thought I had discovered a secret passageway."

"But instead you discovered us," Jason replied. In that instant, he decided that he could trust this girl. He blurted out, "I know this might sound like a really, really dorky question, but, um, where are we?"

"We are in a storage room of the House of Visitors, as you can see," replied the girl, surprised by the question.

Rick was not as trusting as Jason. "Yes, of course," he said quickly. "The House of Visitors. We had been exploring, you see." He gestured to the hole in the wall. "There's nothing back there, nothing interesting, anyway."

"Yeah," Jason said. "There's really no reason to check it out. Too bad you didn't find a secret passageway," he went on, forcing a laugh.

The girl eyed them suspiciously. "Who are you?"

"We're, um, visitors!" Rick said.

"Yeah, visitors!" Jason agreed. "And so we came to the right place, didn't we? The House of Visitors! It only makes sense, right?"

The girl's face brightened. "Do you mean that you came here with the great fleet?"

Jason was uncertain how to respond. But Rick jumped in, "Yes, we came with the fleet."

"That is wonderful news!" the girl exclaimed. "I did not realize that boys my age were coming, too. I thought the fleet was only bringing over the same boring old court officials. Anyway, forgive me. I have lost my manners. I should have known that you were foreigners who have traveled a long distance."

"You've got that right," Jason muttered under his breath.

The girl seemed drawn to the hole in the wall. She stepped toward it cautiously.

Rick piped up. "How about if we try to hide this hole?" he suggested. "So, like, you don't get in trouble or anything?"

"Oh yes, thank you!" the girl said eagerly.

The three kids got to work. They found a long board the shape of a crescent moon, which, according to the girl, was a discarded bed. They pushed it up against the wall, covering the hole from view.

The whole time, Rick's thoughts were on Julia. *Was she okay? Would she return and try to find them?* But with this girl around, he was afraid to say anything to Jason.

"Much better," the girl said, admiring their work. "As long as no one moves this aside, the hole will remain our secret. And if we leave soon, I will not be caught by my father." She paused, then asked, "Will you come with me as my guests?"

Jason bit his lip, thinking. "Sure, yes," he finally replied. "It would be an honor. Thank you."

"Just give us a few minutes to discuss things," Rick added. "I mean, if that's all right with you."

The girl nodded politely and smiled. "Yes, but please hurry. This is not a place where I am supposed to be." She moved across the room and opened the door. "I will wait for you outside."

"Great, thanks," Jason said. "We'll be out in a jiffy."

As soon as the girl had walked out of the room, Rick quickly collected their things in a bundle: the *Dictionary of Forgotten Languages*, Ulysses Moore's diary, the candles, some matches, and the rope.

"What about Julia?" he asked Jason. "What do you think? I feel like we just shut her out on the other side of the wall. If we leave now, we might be putting her in danger."

Jason shook his head. "You said yourself that you saw Julia open the door," he said. "She's safe. I know it."

Rick frowned.

"Look," Jason said, "I'm her twin brother. Julia and I have a special connection. I'd know if she was in trouble."

Rick wasn't entirely convinced. "Tell you what, let's leave her a message." He picked up a broken piece of clay from one of the smashed jars and scrawled a message on the wall.

"Please!" the girl called from outside the door. "We must hurry."

"Oh yeah, sure!" Jason answered. He hurried to the door, glancing back at Rick. The boy from Kilmore Cove was finishing writing on the wall:

JC, DON'T MOVE!
WE'LL BE BACK!

Then he added:

JASON WAS RIGHT.
WE REALLY ARE IN EGYPT!

Back in the old stone room of Argo Manor, Nestor had convinced Julia to sit down on the sofa. He wrapped a blanket around her shoulders. The girl seemed to be in shock. It had all happened so fast that she had not realized she was the only one to cross back through the threshold.

Why had she run away? She struggled to remember exactly what had happened. Nestor gently prodded her for every fact, every detail — anything that would give him a clue as to the boys' whereabouts.

"There was an explosion, you say?" Nestor inquired patiently.

Julia clasped her hands on top of her head. "There was a stairway leading up to a wall. And we heard banging," she recalled. "It sounded like something was behind it — or like someone was pounding on it. Then Jason started knocking and then . . . then there was a crash and a big cloud of dust."

Julia looked up at Nestor, fright still in her eyes. "Somebody shouted, 'Run! Run!' I didn't look back — I should have looked back — but I just ran, Nestor, I just ran as fast as I could. I came to the door and opened it. . . ."

"And here you are," Nestor murmured.

"Yes," Julia said. "Here I am. But I thought it would bring me back to the grotto. How could the door lead me here?"

Nestor nodded grimly. If he knew the answer to that question, he was not saying.

Julia felt something in her pocket. It was the four keys — she still had them! Absently, she placed them on the table in front of her, her hands still trembling.

"The door is mysterious," Nestor said thoughtfully. "So much is still unknown."

"Wait," Julia suddenly said, as if newly alert. "You already know about this door?"

Nestor made a dismissive gesture. "That's not what I meant," he said.

"You know!" Julia said accusingly. "You know all about this door!"

Nestor raised an eyebrow and tried to change the subject. "You are upset," he said. "In shock, probably. Let me make you some tea."

"No!" Julia cried. "Answer me! My brother is back there. My friend is back there. Tell me what you know about this door! Were we really in Egypt? How did I end up back here?"

Nestor stood up. "I will go make you some nice

hot tea," he said soothingly. He disappeared into
the kitchen.

"Nestor? Where are you going? Nestor!" Julia
called after him.

The old man did not answer. Julia stood unsteadily,
her thoughts cloudy. She walked to the door and
tried to open it, pushing and pulling. She tried the
keys, but they didn't work. It was sealed shut.

"I will go make you some nice hot tea," she grumbled, imitating Nestor. "I hate tea. It's a drink for
old ladies and . . . and their mothers!" she muttered.
"I don't want tea. I want my brother!"

She fumbled once more with the keys, frantically
trying to open the door.

"It's no use," Nestor said kindly. He had
reentered the room. "It won't open."

Julia felt a wave of anger surging within her. She
furiously slid the four keys, one after the other, into
the locks in the correct order.

O-P-E-N.

First the owl, then the porcupine, then the elephant, and then the newt.

"Please, Julia," Nestor said in a soft voice. "We
cannot open the door." He watched her for a minute longer, then turned and left the room.

Julia gritted her teeth. She turned the keys, yanked

on the door, and pushed against it with all her strength. But it would not move.

She tried again and again. Finally, she collapsed on the floor, exhausted. The old man was right. The door would not open.

She found Nestor in the kitchen, waiting patiently. His hands were wrapped around a mug of tea. Another cup, beside a plate of toast and jam, was set across the table from him, before an empty chair.

"Sit," Nestor said quietly. "Eat."

Julia did not speak for a long time. She ate the toast and was surprised at how hungry she was. Nestor poured her a bowl of soup, which she ate in silence.

"Why won't it open?" Julia finally asked. "What do you know about that door, Nestor? Where are Jason and Rick?"

Nestor shrugged his shoulders. There was kindness in his eyes. "You have many questions," he said. "I could not possibly answer all of them — if, that is, I even knew the answers."

"I don't understand," Julia said, exasperated. "You talk in riddles. Everything around here is a lousy riddle. Why can't you just speak plain English?" she demanded. "What did we do to deserve this? Did we make some kind of terrible mistake?"

Julia's eyes began to well with tears, and she cursed herself for showing weakness.

Nestor gathered the dishes and brought them to the sink. He moved slowly, calmly. He placed a napkin for Julia on the table, but did not comment about her tears.

"You are tired," he said. "It has been a long, long day."

"Yeah, that's the understatement of the century," Julia said.

Nestor smiled. "Such wit, such courage," he told her. "Even now, you cannot help but be clever and oh so very brave."

He placed a hand on Julia's cheek. "Listen to me," he said softly. "You have not done anything wrong. In truth, I am very relieved that you are here with me, safe and sound. We shall see this through, you and I, together. But for now, you should rest. We'll have much to do tomorrow."

Julia nodded. She didn't want to sleep — she wanted answers. But she was too exhausted to argue anymore. So she let Nestor lead her to the couch on the portico. There, she curled up and, almost instantly, fell asleep.

- Chapter 5 -
MARUK

The House
of Life??

After leading Rick and Jason through a series of dark hallways, the Egyptian girl paused. "My name is Maruk," she told them awkwardly.

Jason smiled. "It's nice to meet you, Maruk. I'm Jason and he's . . . *gone*? Where'd Rick go?"

Rick came running up to them. "Sorry, I, uh, stopped to look at something," he explained. What Rick did not say was that he had been secretly marking the walls along the way as a precaution in case the boys had to find their way back alone.

Rick held out his hand. "I'm Rick."

Maruk gave them a funny look. "What peculiar names," she said. "Jason and Rick. Are you Nubian?"

"Not exactly," Jason answered.

"That is good," Maruk replied. "My father does not think highly of Nubians."

Rick didn't like the sound of Maruk's father, and he wasn't looking forward to meeting any adults before he and Jason had figured some things out.

Maruk persisted with her questioning. "If you are not Nubian, then where do you come from . . . *exactly*? Your skin is fair. Are you Phoenicians, Minoans, Semites? Libyans?"

"It's difficult to explain," Rick offered. "Let's just say we come from very, very, very far away."

"The truth is, I'm English and he's Irish," Jason interrupted.

Rick shot him a disapproving look.

"Irish?" Maruk said, struggling over the unfamiliar word.

"My family is originally from Ireland," Rick explained, having been left no choice in the matter. "It is an island. Jason is from an island, too, but it is much larger, called England."

Maruk shook her head. "That must be very far away indeed, for I have never heard of such places. You must show me on a map."

"You mean," Jason said, "you've never even heard of England? Fish and chips? The Beatles? David Beckham? Manchester United? Monty Python?"

Maruk laughed. "Such strange boys you are," she said. "Ah, here we are." And with those words, the three companions entered a vast garden surrounded by massive, towering walls. They were dotted with gaps and openings through which gulls, high above, flapped and fluttered.

"Oh . . . wow," Jason gasped.

Maruk smiled, enjoying their amazement. She was proud of her city. She led the boys to the center of the garden, to a group of palm trees, swishing canes, and pools of water. Then she turned down a wide, earthen avenue lined with small sphinxes, each holding the curved pole of a parasol that shaded the lane.

The boys were stunned by the incredible sights.

"I feel like I'm Veruca Salt wandering around in Willy Wonka's chocolate factory," Rick said.

"You mean we can eat this stuff?" Jason joked. Then he turned serious. "I know what you mean, Rick. Now I know what Alice must have felt, falling down the rabbit hole. We're in Wonderland."

"Jason, where are we? How can this be real?" whispered Rick. The avenue opened into a field covered with flower beds in full bloom. Herons and ibises with long beaks strolled about lazily.

"I'm not sure," Jason answered. "But I've never imagined, in all my dreams, that anywhere could look like this."

Maruk smiled mischievously. "Come along, you two."

And they followed. After all, she was their guide — and they were on an incredible journey.

"Now I must stop for a moment to visit my teacher," Maruk told the boys. "After that, I can introduce you to the Great Master Scribe."

"The Great Master Scribe?" Rick repeated.

"Yes," Maruk replied. "But I prefer to call him Father."

Rick touched Jason's elbow. Casting a worried look at his friend, he said in a hushed voice, "I don't have a good feeling about this."

Maruk paused before a statue that towered twenty feet above them. It was in the shape of a man with the head of a baboon, holding some kind of writing instrument in his hand.

"Here is a tribute to the god Thoth," Maruk explained, casually gesturing to the great statue. She turned and headed toward a square building, leaving the boys alone to gaze at the statue in wonder.

Rick quietly opened the dictionary and read to Jason:

Thoth: ancient Egyptian divinity who taught writing and mathematics to mankind.

"Oh please, don't tell me that we've traveled thousands of years into the past only to wind up back in school," Jason groaned.

Rick grinned. "Actually, I've always been pretty good at math."

"Figures." Jason sighed.

They caught up with Maruk in front of the building, and they all stood admiring the hieroglyphs that decorated its facade.

Strangely, Rick could *read* the hieroglyphs. "Dwelling of the Scribes," he said aloud.

Jason looked at him in amazement. "I can read it,

too," he confided. "I don't know anything about hieroglyphics. Yet somehow I can look at these and understand exactly what they say. How is that possible, Rick?"

"How is it possible?" Rick repeated, waving his arms around. "How is any of this possible?"

"Well, I guess there's only one thing to do," Jason decided.

"Yeah, what's that?"

"Buckle up and enjoy the ride!"

Inside the Dwelling of the Scribes, the air was cool and dark. There were people milling about, busy at a variety of tasks. But the moment they noticed Maruk and her friends, they bowed their heads.

Rick and Jason were stunned. They bowed their heads in return, instinctively knowing that it was the proper response. Rick asked Maruk, "Is your father some kind of really important person?"

"Yeah, like a big shot?" Jason added.

Maruk laughed. "A big shot? What a funny expression." She tossed her braid over her shoulder and lifted her chin slightly. "Except for the Pharaoh and the High Priest, my father is the most important person in our land."

Jason whistled. "That's a big shot, all right."

Rick gulped, growing increasingly nervous about

meeting Maruk's father. How could they explain who they were, or how they had come here?

They made their way down a narrow hallway until they reached a large, open area where water cascaded down from the ceiling. It collected in a central basin decorated with light-blue tiles.

"This is the water hall," Maruk explained. "Down there are the writing halls. And over there, the flower pools — so beautiful, you must visit them one day! And at the top of those stairs is the terrace. Please await me there. I'll meet you as soon as I can."

"You're leaving us?" Jason asked.

"Just for a moment," Maruk replied. "I am a student here. I must see my teacher. Do not be alarmed. I will be back soon and then I will bring you to meet my father."

"The big shot," Jason said with a smile.

Maruk laughed. "Yes, Master of the Scribes — and one of Egypt's biggest big shots!"

Back at Argo Manor, Julia awoke on the couch in the portico. Nestor had placed a pillow under her head and a large quilt over her legs. The mysterious caretaker sat nearby. As she woke up he nodded at her.

Had she been dreaming? Was none of it real? The keys, the door, the wall? But soon it all came crashing back to her. Jason and Rick, trapped on the other side.

It had not been a dream.

"It was Egypt," Julia said aloud.

"Egypt, yes, of course," the old man replied. His voice was gentle. He seemed sincere, not mocking. "And how did you come to arrive in Egypt?"

Julia told him their story, every detail she could remember, from the beginning. The round room, the long stairway, Jason's leap across darkness, the chute, the grotto lit by fireflies, the *Metis*.

Through it all, Nestor nodded thoughtfully. He never spoke, never asked questions; he simply listened.

"Jason was the one who figured out how to make it work," Julia told him.

At this, Nestor smiled. "Jason, of course," he commented. "Please continue."

"We opened the grotto door, the one with three turtles above it," Julia said. "There was a weird hallway covered with sand. Like it was a beach or a desert or something. The air was suddenly hot and dry. We found a stairway. We heard voices and that's when Jason told us we were in Egypt — ancient Egypt."

Nestor raised an eyebrow. "Jason told you this?"

Julia nodded. "He, like, *knew*. It was weird. I can't explain it. Anyway, we were walking and there was knocking at the wall, like someone trying to send us a message. Jason knocked back. That's when the wall collapsed. It felt like the roof was falling down." Julia brought a hand to her neck. "I felt like I was in a mine, you know, and it was caving in all around me. I had to escape. I just ran, Nestor. I never looked back."

Nestor sipped his tea and did not comment.

Julia suddenly sat up. "What am I doing? Sitting here, jabbering to you? I have to call my parents," she announced. "Jason is missing. They need to be here. They have to come home." She stood and crossed into the sitting room, where she found the telephone.

Nestor watched as she left. For the first time, deep concern showed on his face.

Julia struggled with the phone, dropping it once. She had difficulty dialing, her fingers trembling. "What am I supposed to do?" she cried out. "Nobody here is helping me! I lost my brother and I don't understand any of this."

Julia felt herself struggling to breathe. She was panicked, frightened, and confused. "Help me," she whispered. "Jason, where are you?"

Nestor appeared in the archway. At that moment, he looked to Julia like the saddest man alive.

He picked up an object off a shelf. "See this," he said to Julia. "A shrunken Moor's head. It is from the bazaar in the Land of Punt, in ancient Egypt. I am told this is more than three thousand years old." He stared directly into Julia's eyes. "Mr. Moore brought it home after his third trip to Egypt . . . aboard the *Metis*. Do you understand?"

Julia blinked. *He knows*, she thought.

Nestor picked up a different object. "This wooden case has engravings that, according to legend, were copied from the Book of the Dead — a religious text that is now impossible to find. Julia, it is five thousand years old. This case was purchased, after lengthy negotiations, by Mrs. Moore during her sixth trip to the Land of Punt aboard the *Metis*.

"Now do you understand?"

Julia blinked again, sniffed, and nodded. "I'm getting the picture," she said, hanging up the phone. "Ulysses Moore . . ." she began. "The diary. It wasn't a fantasy. It was real. He was there, too."

Nestor nodded sagely. "Yes," he said. "He was there. Many, many times. In fact, many of the items that you see in this house came from the journeys that Ulysses Moore and his wife made aboard the *Metis*."

Julia followed Nestor back into the stone room. They paused before the scarred and battered old door.

"You never went with them?" Julia asked.

Nestor smiled, and seemed to pause thoughtfully. "No, never. My place was here, in this world."

Julia observed Nestor closely. From the beginning, her sense of him had always been that he was holding back the truth, keeping secrets from her. Even now, when he claimed to reveal all, the story came only in bits and pieces. She did not trust him, not completely. But at the same time, she realized that Nestor had answers. He might be the key to Jason's safe return.

"Didn't Ulysses ever ask you to come along?" she persisted.

Nestor chuckled. "Oh, certainly. In particular, Mrs. Moore often asked me to come aboard the *Metis* with them. If only you knew how she went on and on, trying to convince me. But, no, those adventures are not for me," Nestor said. "I like things that stay in their place, like trees and rocks."

"Tell me about Ulysses," Julia demanded.

"Ulysses Moore was a traveler," the caretaker of Argo Manor said, warming to the subject. "Travelers aren't vacationers. They aren't merely visitors, either. No," his eyes brightened, "they are adventurers, risk-takers, daredevils."

He continued, "To truly travel you must have a base, the place you set off from. And then, of course, you need to return to prepare for your next journey. As Ulysses said, 'No circle is without a center. And no journey is without a return.'" Nestor smiled as if struck by a memory. "Ulysses Moore was talking, of course, about the greatest journey of all — death."

"Death?" Julia repeated. A few hairs raised on the back of her neck. "How can anyone return from death?"

Nestor shook his head. "It is impossible, of course," he admitted. "But Ulysses spoke of it often. He was very intelligent, that man. And he loved this house more than anything in the world. This house, and his beautiful wife, Penelope."

"What was she like?" Julia asked.

"A sweet woman," Nestor told her. "Always there to help. Kindhearted. But, like her husband, full of dreams and a thirst for adventure."

Julia nodded, thinking that she would have liked Penelope if they had met. "And you?" she asked. "How long have you been at Argo Manor?"

Nestor waved his hand as if swatting away the question. "Oh, who can remember? I feel like I've lived here forever. I mean, in the caretaker's cottage, naturally." He returned to the subject of Ulysses

Moore and his wife. "They crossed through that door many times," he said. "They would be gone for a week, two weeks, sometimes months at a time. And I would stay here awaiting their return."

"They must have been an amazing couple," Julia said.

"Yes, they were," Nestor agreed. "Ulysses and Penny — that is, Penelope — Moore."

Julia caught Nestor's slip. "Penny?" she questioned.

"Oh, well, he called her that sometimes. Penny this and Penny that," Nestor said with a chuckle.

"Strange that there are no photos of them," Julia mused. "And strange, too, that the portrait of Ulysses Moore is missing from the top of the stairs," she said.

Nestor eyed her thoughtfully. He snapped his fingers. "Oh yes, the portrait! Mr. Moore ordered it burned — God, how he hated to see himself in photos or pictures. Very peculiar that way, I must admit. It got even worse after Penelope . . . passed away."

"How did she die?" Julia asked.

Nestor paused before answering, as if deciding whether to answer at all. "The cliff," he said. "She fell off the cliff."

– Chapter 6 –
A RIDDLE

...Even if I find one key, it won't be enough.... There are four locks!

Jason and Rick climbed the stairs and walked out onto the high terrace. From there, for the first time, they could begin to comprehend the layout of their surroundings. On the other side of the protective walls was a large, vibrant city teeming with life. It stretched out like a great giant, its fingertips touching a large body of water.

"The Nile?" Jason wondered.

"No, smell the air," Rick replied. "Look at the gulls. Look at the waves, flowing to the shore and ebbing out again. It isn't a river, Jason. It's the sea."

The two travelers drank in their surroundings, their hearts pounding.

"Why are we here?" Rick asked.

Jason could not answer at first. Instead, he took Ulysses Moore's diary from their bundle of belongings and leafed through the pages. Finally, he said, "I think the old owner of Argo Manor wanted this to happen." He turned to a page that depicted Tutankhamen's death mask. Below it were the words: *The Pharaoh's treasure.*

"When I was at the helm of the *Metis*, back when we were in the grotto, this picture is what I was thinking about," Jason confessed to Rick. "I held it in my mind, this picture of the child pharaoh, and I wished it to be real."

Rick listened thoughtfully. "But why?" he repeated. "There must be a reason. There must be a logical explanation. Why us? Why here?"

"We don't know why," Jason said. "It's the hand we've been dealt. But I know this: We have to see it through to the end. There's no going back until we solve the riddle — the riddle of *why?*"

Jason turned to another page and showed the diary to Rick. In tiny, angular handwriting, Ulysses Moore had described a place called the Land of Punt. A pencil sketch faithfully depicted the parasol-lined avenue of the sphinxes, the same avenue that the boys had walked down to reach the Dwelling of the Scribes.

"He's been here," Rick said in a hushed voice. "You knew that, didn't you?"

Jason tilted his head from side to side. "I've suspected it ever since we set foot in the grotto, yes. We aren't the first ones. Ulysses Moore and his wife came here, aboard the *Metis*, just like we did."

Rick read the notes in the notebook. "Old Ulysses wrote that *the city is a place greatly loved by the pharaohs, who, attracted by its beauty, made frequent expeditions to visit it.*" He scanned the next page and read aloud: "*Punt is a lost city of the African continent — a legendary city that no archeologist has ever succeeded in finding.*"

"Does he say anything about those gigantic walls?" Jason asked.

Rick turned a few pages. "Oh yes! Here it says that *the greatest treasure in all of Punt is stored within these walls, which are really a maze of stairs and hallways, pits and towers, with tunnels and passageways leading off in every direction — even deep underground . . .*"

Jason stared at the walls, his eyes wide in appreciation.

Rick flipped more pages with Jason peering over his shoulder. "Somewhere in this garden is the entrance to the labyrinth," Rick said. "It is a temple called the House of Life, which is dedicated to the god Thoth. Stored within this vast stone maze is the Collection, which supposedly contains all of the knowledge of the ancient world."

Rick continued poring over the pages. Again he read aloud: "*Punt is a location sought out by all the travelers of antiquity, for anything of value can be found inside its walls. Every day, in its markets, at its port, or along its caravan route, travelers exchange goods of all kinds: scrolls, amber, incense, gold, ivory, quartz — every treasure known to mankind.*"

Rick pointed to the page. "Hey, check it out — a map of the city!"

"And look," Jason said, his voice full of excitement, "some places have been circled."

On the facing page, written in what looked like a hasty scrawl, were these words:

To get your bearings you will need
Good fortune and lucky stars.
Seek out the map in the tower
Under the four wands.

Jason looked at Rick. "What the . . . ?"

Suddenly, Maruk's voice threaded up the stairs, calling their names.

Rick hurriedly tucked the notebook away. "What do we do?" he whispered.

"For now, let's stick with Maruk. She seems to know her way around," Jason said. "We'll make up the rest as we go along."

Maruk led the boys to the grand entrance of the House of Life, where her father worked. Two great statues held up its architrave. Each step in the grand staircase leading inside was painted a different color. Crossing over the threshold, they found themselves engulfed by an endless swarm of people, busily moving in all directions. Jason almost felt like he was back at Waterloo Station in London during

rush hour. For Rick, who was used to the simple life in Kilmore Cove, it was overwhelming.

Jason seemed to notice Rick's discomfort. "It's all right," he whispered. "Just act like you belong. It's a big city. No one will notice us."

They crossed through the enormous room, passing entrances to corridors, passageways, and stairways that led to higher levels — turning, twisting, leading up and down between the Grand Entrance and the other rooms.

"It's like we're in the center of an ant farm," Rick commented. "Tunnels go in every direction."

In the center of the vast room, a vertical pit as wide as an Olympic swimming pool made its way down into the ground, revealing hundreds of other staircases, corridors, and passageways. Wooden carts carrying papyrus scrolls and people squeaked up and down along the walls of the pit.

Jason and Rick's senses were struck by both the amazing sights and all the incredible smells that drifted through the hot, musty air: leather, macerated papyrus, cinnamon, and nutmeg.

"Welcome to the Collection," Maruk said solemnly.

"And what, exactly, do you collect?" Rick asked, turning his body to avoid a large basket full of scrolls that was being pulled up out of the pit.

Maruk shrugged, her eyes gleaming. "Everything, anything," she answered. "Writings, rolls of papyrus, tablets. But also statues, furniture, craftsmen's tools, coins. We collect our history, our culture. Everything that documents our great civilization, we keep here and protect."

So why haven't I ever heard of this place before? Jason wondered, gazing at the scene before him in awe. He watched hardworking men climb the stairs, up and up, until they became as tiny as insects, or descend down into the ground below until they were swallowed by the darkness. Rick was right. It really *was* like an elaborate ant farm.

"Your father is in charge of all this?" Rick asked, baffled and impressed.

"Yes," Maruk replied proudly. "Come!"

The girl led her new friends to a dark corner between several statues, where two men stood. The men wore identical purple tunics and tall headdresses each adorned with a single white feather. They bowed to Maruk as she approached.

"Honorable Indexers," Maruk greeted them. "My friends and I wish to meet with the Great Master Scribe in his chambers."

The taller of the two men, who was thin and sinewy with pointed features, cleared his throat and raised an eyebrow. "I am sorry, Maruk, but Rule

Number Thirty-two forbids us from granting your wish."

Maruk frowned. "And what would Rule Number Thirty-two be?"

"Pay no heed to children," said the shorter man, who was decidedly plump.

Maruk planted her hands on her hips. "I am the eldest daughter of the Great Master Scribe!"

The taller man stared down at Maruk. "Forgive us. We realize who you are. But nonetheless, it is beyond our means to grant your wish."

"And why is that?" Maruk asked sharply.

"Rule Number Four: The Pharaoh's security must be of utmost importance," the short, plump man said.

The tall Indexer nodded appreciatively. "The Pharaoh could arrive for his visit any moment now. Did you not notice all the agitation in the House of Life? We are working very hard to get everything in order. We have received strict orders. Rule Number Fifty-Six: No one is to enter the House of Life until further notice."

Maruk looked more determined than ever. "We must visit my father's chambers."

"Ah, indeed, the chambers of the Great Master Scribe," the shorter man replied. "But my dear girl, according to Rule Number . . ."

"For all I care," Maruk said, "you may stick your rules in your hats! I need to see my father!"

The Indexers stepped back, shocked and, it seemed, slightly fearful. The plump one's lower lip began to tremble. The tall one yielded, but only slightly. "In that case, you may go. However," he added sharply, "your friends cannot."

"And why not?" Maruk demanded.

"Rule Number Twelve: No guests may enter until further orders."

Maruk stood firm. "But it is I who am ordering you to let them enter," she demanded.

The tall Indexer's eyes narrowed. He turned to his partner. "Pepi, please tell her about Rule Number Eight."

Pepi stood at full attention. "Rule Number Eight," he recited. "Each guest must carry a pass at all times."

Maruk huffed and turned to Rick and Jason, who stood watching this exchange with open mouths. "They are always like this," she confided with a grin. "But they can be outsmarted."

Clearly, Maruk had not yet given up the fight. In fact, Jason noted, she seemed to enjoy it. "You are, of course, correct, Master Micerinus. My compliments to you, too, Pepi. My father will be pleased to hear of your excellent work."

Micerinus and Pepi nodded with satisfaction.

"There may even be a reward in store for you," Maruk said. "If, that is, I could find some way to let him know about your stalwart resolution."

Pepi smiled sagely. "Ah, but a rule is a rule. . . ."

"True," Micerinus interrupted greedily, "but there are always exceptions."

"Please tell me about these exceptions," Maruk prodded. "As you said yourself, my guests need passes if they wish to enter."

The Indexers whispered together for a few brief moments. Finally, they turned back to Maruk. "There is a rule that you may find favor with," Micerinus said.

Maruk raised her eyebrows at him questioningly.

"Rule Number something-or-other," Micerinus said quietly. His eyes scanned the room, making sure no one could overhear. He stepped aside, and bowed deeply. "Please enter, dear lady, fine gentlemen. Visit your father, Master of the Scribes. And be sure to mention the work of two excellent Indexers . . . Micerinus and Pepi!"

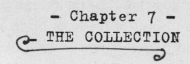

- Chapter 7 -
THE COLLECTION

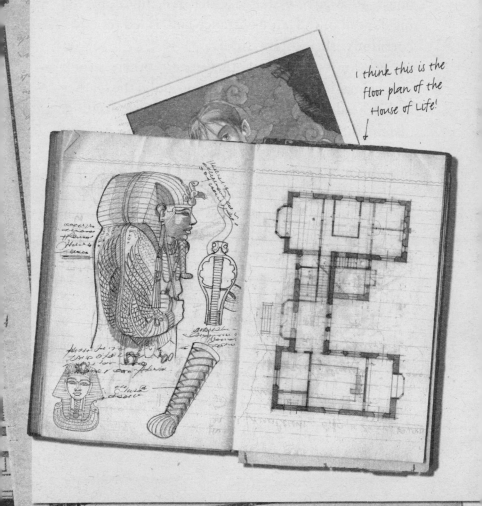

I think this is the
floor plan of the
House of Life!

Micerinus and Pepi issued Jason and Rick two scarab beetles made of black stone — passes that would permit them to explore the Collection freely.

The Indexers accompanied Maruk and her two guests to a narrow staircase that rose up along the inside wall of the large entrance hall. It led to a tiny corridor with a sloping floor.

"We know shortcuts that many others could barely imagine," Micerinus said proudly, the feather in his headdress brushing against the low ceiling. "Right this way, honored guests. We shall accompany you for a short distance before returning to our important tasks."

The corridor was bathed in a soft light reflected by an ingenious system of mirrors. The walls were painted ocher yellow. In some places, they were lined with pigeonholes of different sizes that contained rolls of papyrus, wooden tablets, and idols.

Rick noticed that each pigeonhole was marked with a symbol or a number or both. He imagined it helped the scribes keep track of the vast number of items in the collection. The little group entered a circular area with a high skylight. To Rick, it was like looking up from the bottom of a long smokestack. They turned again into yet another corridor, then came to two passageways that moved off in opposite directions. Micerinus confidently took the one on their right, which was far steeper than the other.

Rick walked beside Pepi. Though he dreaded drawing attention to himself, Rick could no longer contain his curiosity. "What is your job here?" Rick asked the portly apprentice. "Do you handle security?"

Pepi chuckled, while looking straight ahead. "Security is handled by the guards, who are far more formidable than I, believe me."

Micerinus added, "Our job is to remember what is stored within the Collection." He pointed distractedly at the pigeonholes on either side of the corridor. "Each container holds an item. It is only the Indexers who know what it is and how it may be found. We pass down our knowledge to our apprentices, generation after generation."

"Orally?" Rick asked. "Isn't it written down?"

Micerinus sniffed. "Writing things down weakens the memory. If a paper is lost, all is forgotten."

Rick scratched his head. "But there are thousands of niches here! You mean to tell me that each Indexer knows every one of them?"

"No, certainly not," Micerinus replied. "That would

be impossible. Each Indexer is assigned a building and a specific number of rooms. He is responsible only for those niches that are entrusted to him."

"How big is this place, anyway?" Rick wondered. "The Collection is divided into twenty-two buildings," Micerinus explained. "Each building has twenty-two rooms. Each room has twenty-two corridors. And each corridor has . . ."

". . . twenty-two niches?" Rick guessed.

Micerinus stopped and stared at Rick. "Why on earth should there be twenty-two niches?" he snapped scornfully. "It has fifty-six. Or one hundred and twelve. Or one hundred and sixty-eight. And so on."

"Touchy, isn't he?" Jason murmured to Rick.

"This pertains only to the Collection Above, obviously," Micerinus added.

"Obviously," Jason echoed, looking puzzled.

Pepi continued the explanation. "Then you must consider the underground corridors. And there are many, many more below than there are above."

"Ah, here we are," Micerinus said at last. "We will leave you here, for we must get back to our stations. To reach the chambers of the Great Master Scribe, simply take the corridor there and follow it straight down without turning. You will reach the pyramid in the blink of an eye."

Maruk thanked the Indexers, and handed them each a coin.

Before they left, Micerinus issued a warning. "Beware," he said, pointing a finger at all three of them. "Nothing in the niches is to be touched without the assistance of an Indexer."

"We understand," Maruk replied.

"And don't forget," Pepi added cheerfully, "if you hear the sounding of trumpets, you must immediately abandon the House of Life."

"Or what happens?" Jason asked. "We turn into pumpkins?"

"You will be arrested by the guards," Micerinus snapped. "That is something you would not enjoy, believe me. They are not so kind as Pepi and I."

The three kids walked on, suddenly apprehensive without the Indexers at their side. At least that's how Jason and Rick felt. Maruk strode confidently, familiar with her surroundings, having visited her father countless times.

"It must be easy to get lost around here," Jason remarked.

"Oh yes, it is like a great labyrinth, an endless maze," Maruk confirmed. "One must be careful."

"Has anyone ever explored the entire Collection?" Rick asked.

"My father has attempted it," the girl replied, brushing her hand along the marble wall. "But I suspect that it is an impossible task. There are corridors that nobody has set foot in for many years. The Abandoned Corridors."

Maruk made a gesture in the air as if to ward off bad luck.

"Do you mean the ones underground?" Rick guessed.

"In that giant pit thing we saw when we entered?" Jason added.

"You have much to learn, my friends," Maruk replied. "That is the Collection Below. According to legend, the Abandoned Corridors are in the upper levels."

Maruk stopped to look at her friends. Her eyes gleamed with a strange nervousness. "Years ago, a terrible fire broke out in those corridors. Two Indexers, a husband and wife, were never found again. Not even their charred remains were left behind. They were engulfed in the fire, along with everything that was being stored in that section."

"A husband and a wife," mused Jason.

Maruk started walking again. "Their story is told in a famous song, 'The Ballad of Two Lovers.'"

"I don't know that one," Jason said. "Can you hum a few bars?"

Maruk did not get his little joke. She replied, "It is a song about two lovers who have been wandering these corridors for hundreds of years, looking for each other without ever being reunited."

"While we, on the other hand," Rick said apprehensively, "know exactly where we're going . . . right?"

"More or less," Maruk said with a shrug. "I've never come from this direction before. Micerinus's shortcuts are impressive."

A hundred steps farther down, the corridor opened into a more spacious area. The kids found themselves inside what appeared to be a perfect pyramid.

"And here we are," Maruk announced, pleased. "This is where my father works."

The room was simple and elegant at the same time. Linen curtains billowed in the breeze, draping down from the ceiling like the sails of a ship. Two wide openings stood on either side of the walls, allowing for the flow of air. Arranged in the center of the room were four tables that held a variety of ancient objects. Against the back wall there were niches similar to the ones in the corridors, each one marked with a different symbol. Against the opposite wall lay scrolls of papyrus, like gigantic spools of thread.

"Father?" Maruk called out.

There was no reply.

Maruk walked around the four tables, and called out once again. And again, there was no answer.

"I guess nobody's home," Jason said.

"Maybe that's a good thing," Rick whispered to Jason. "I have a feeling we should get out of here before her father shows up and starts asking questions."

A woman came into the room from the other entranceway.

"Maruk!" she exclaimed. "What are you doing here?"

The girl turned and motioned to her two friends at her side.

"Your father has been called away," the woman said. "He has gone to welcome the Pharaoh."

Jason and Rick looked at her and smiled politely. She wore a long white gown, and her posture was both stiff and elegant at the same time. Her left arm was cradled in a sling looped around her neck and shoulder. With each word she spoke, her right arm made a graceful gesture.

Maruk whispered to her friends, "My father's assistant lost the use of her arm during the fire I told you about before. She has lost her memory, too, because she took a horrible blow to the head. So she sometimes says things that seem a bit strange. Please forgive her. She is as harmless as a flower."

"When will my father return?" Maruk asked the woman in a louder voice.

"That depends upon the Pharaoh. If you wish to wait for him here, perhaps you might catch a glimpse of young Tutankhamen," the assistant replied.

"Tutankhamen?" Jason asked excitedly. "He's coming here?" And to Rick he whispered, "What did I tell you? I knew there was a connection between him and this place!"

The woman smiled. "Maruk, who are your friends? I have never seen them before."

"They arrived with the ships," Maruk replied.

"You came with the fleet?" the woman asked.

"Yes," Jason said reluctantly. "Isn't that right, Rick?"

Rick stared at the middle-aged woman. Maruk was right, she appeared as harmless, and as lovely, as a flower.

"I said, isn't that right?" Jason repeated.

"Oh yes, we came here with the fleet," Rick confirmed.

"Magnificent," the woman said cheerfully. "And on which ship did you sail?" she asked, gesturing to the objects on the table.

Only then did Rick notice that the objects were a vast collection of model ships, both small and large.

Noticing his amazement, Maruk walked up to him.

"Do you like them, Rick? My father makes them. It is his hobby and his passion," she explained.

Rick gazed at the models on the table. He was immediately struck by their uncanny similarity to the ones he had seen in the tower room at Argo Manor.

A shiver ran down his spine. Meanwhile, the woman waited for an answer to her query.

"We came in this one," Rick finally replied. He pointed at a ship that looked like an exact copy of the *Nefertiti's Eye*, a model ship in Ulysses Moore's study back at Argo Manor. In a way, it was not a lie.

"Then you must have been on an incredible journey," the woman said.

"Oh yes, it certainly was incredible," Rick echoed, suddenly feeling dazed and confused. He lifted up the model of *Nefertiti's Eye* and handed it to Jason, who murmured, "It's impossible . . . impossible."

The woman laughed happily. "You are impressed by the Great Master Scribe's talents. He will be pleased to know that you admire his work so much."

"His work is perfect," Rick answered. "Everything is exactly right, down to the smallest detail."

Maruk, too, was pleased by Rick's reaction. "Father works on these models endlessly, long into the night," she explained. "At every spare moment, he sits down at the table over there and picks up his tools. He says that while he works on small things, he can concentrate on bigger issues. Isn't that right?" she added, turning toward the woman.

"Your father often says that he wishes he had more time so he could finish the entire fleet," the woman answered. "His latest model has taken him almost a year to complete. Would you boys care to see it?"

Rick and Jason nodded. The woman led them to a workbench, where a model was covered by a cloth. Using only her right hand, she gently lifted off the cloth.

Jason gasped. Rick's feet suddenly felt heavy, as though he were rooted to the floor.

"It is his finest work yet," the woman said with pride.

To their astonishment, Rick and Jason saw that the model was an exact replica of the *Metis*.

- Chapter 8 -
THREE LEAVE, THREE MUST RETURN

The Nefertiti's Eye

"Tell me everything you know about this door," Julia demanded, looking at Nestor. "Everything."

Nestor rubbed his eyes. "I will tell you the truth, Julia. You deserve at least that much. But I'm afraid that my knowledge is limited. I will disappoint you, for I only know what Mr. and Mrs. Moore have told me, and the door was not a subject that they spoke of freely.

"That wall where the door is now, represents the oldest, most ancient wing of Argo Manor. It was here, I believe, even before there was an Argo Manor."

Julia crossed her arms, clearly dissatisfied. "Who built it, Sir Lancelot and the knights of the kitchen table?"

Nestor sighed. "I do not know, Julia," he answered patiently. "I am sorry, but I cannot tell you what I do not know. And," he added, "I am sure that the Moores did not know, either. In fact, I believe one of the reasons why they took those journeys aboard the *Metis* was to find out its secret."

"I don't get it," Julia said, furrowing her brow. "You mean to say that the door has always been here?"

"It's possible," Nestor said with a sigh.

"Hey, sure, I was just walking around in freaking Egypt. So yeah, anything is possible," Julia snapped.

"But none of what you're telling me is helping. I need to know the truth!"

"The truth? Is that all?" Nestor replied. He waved his hands in exasperation. "I don't know what the truth is. No one does. But . . . but," the caretaker repeated, "I do know that Mr. Moore wasn't the first person to live here in Argo Manor. There has always been some sort of dwelling here: a castle, a tower, something. You can find the entire family tree in the library, if you are interested in reading it. This house has been in the Moore family for many, many generations."

"How far back does it go?"

"The family history is complex," Nestor answered. "I have not made a close study of it myself. I do know that the family's last name was once More, with only one *o*. Somewhere along the line a second letter *o* was added to the name, for reasons that are unknown to me."

"You mean the name used to be . . . More . . . like, the opposite of less?" Julia asked.

"Yes, that's one way of looking at it, I suppose. The name is not English in origin. It is derived, I believe, from a Latin word that means custom, tradition, or ancient practice."

"Ancient practice," Julia echoed.

"You can look it up in your dictionary, if you like," Nestor offered.

"I'd love to," Julia replied. "But Rick has the dictionary! Or have you forgotten about my brother and Rick already?"

Nestor suddenly rose to his feet. "It is very late. You are tired, you are angry — and," he said quickly, before Julia could bite his head off again, "you have every right to be angry. However, I think it's best if you get some rest."

Julia gaped at him. "What? Are you kidding me? Jason and Rick are in Egypt! They are trapped somewhere in the . . . in the . . ."

". . . the Land of Punt," Nestor answered calmly. He glanced out the window. The rain was still coming down in sheets.

"Yes," Julia exclaimed. "They're still in the Land of Punt, or Oz, or whatever you want to call it. And you expect me to rest?!"

"It is difficult, I know," Nestor answered.

"I can't rest," Julia said. "We've got to find a way to help them. They could be in danger."

Nestor nodded. "A nice idea," he commented. "Very brave, very noble. I expect nothing less from you. However, you can't help them."

"Why not?"

"As long as they are across the threshold, the door will remain closed to us on this side."

"How do you know that for sure? I don't believe you!" Julia scoffed.

Nestor showed her the burns and scrapes that marked the door. "It has been attempted many times before," he answered. "Believe me when I tell you this. It is not possible to open the door until the travelers have come back home —"

"But *I'm* back!" Julia interrupted.

"Until ALL of the travelers have returned," Nestor added for emphasis, "or until they are no longer able to come back. Three young explorers walked through that door. Three travelers must return before it can be opened again. I am sorry, Julia, but that is how it works."

"So . . . what do we do?" Julia asked, her tone softening.

"We do what I have done for many long years," Nestor answered. "We wait . . . and we hope."

Rick's mind was reeling. There was no denying it: On that table, in ancient Egypt, was the unmistakable form of the craft they had sailed through the storm

inside the grotto of Salton Cliff. And resting on Ulysses Moore's journal in the tower room of Argo Manor was a perfect replica of the *Nefertiti's Eye.*

The two worlds were linked. And the key to that link, the one thing connecting it, was Ulysses Moore.

"That's a really cool ship," Rick commented lamely as the assistant once again covered the model. "I've never seen one like it."

"It is different from the others," the woman told the boys. "This ship is modeled after a drawing. It does not exist in real life."

Jason stared at her, stunned. "A drawing? Are you sure?" he asked. "May we see it?"

The woman gazed at them with an amused expression. "My, your friends are curious!" she said to Maruk. "I know just where it is." She went to the shelves on the back wall and swiftly returned with a long sheet of papyrus.

"This is the drawing," she said, unrolling the scroll.

Inside the papyrus was an ordinary, modern piece of paper, which contained a series of small, intricately detailed sketches of the *Metis* rendered by an exacting hand. The paper looked to Rick as if it had been ripped out of Ulysses Moore's journal.

Jason could not contain himself. "That's a drawing by . . ."

Rick jabbed Jason hard in the ribs.

"Do you recognize this drawing?" the woman asked them.

"Oh no, of course not. How could we?" Rick was quick to answer.

"It's just that, I meant to say," Jason improvised, "that it's a drawing by . . . a really talented artist."

Maruk smiled. "That is what we think, too. It is beautiful, isn't it?"

The woman lightly grazed the paper with her fingers. "I agree," she murmured. "Beautiful and mysterious. There is something special about this drawing. I often find myself staring at it for minutes at a time."

While Maruk and the woman continued to discuss the drawing, Jason pulled Rick aside. "How do you think that paper wound up here?"

"Beats me," Rick said. "I have to tell you, Jason. This whole thing is seriously creeping me out. Maybe we should start thinking about finding our way back home."

"Hold on," Jason said, shushing him. He pretended to admire a small sculpture on a table across the room and spoke in a low voice. "Maruk told us that the House of Life is used to store and protect things. I believe that Ulysses Moore was here, maybe even here in this room."

"But why?" Rick said. "Why come to the House of Life?"

"To store something," Jason answered matter-of-factly. "Or to hide something."

Rick nodded in agreement. "It's possible," he said. "But after today, I'd believe that anything was possible."

"That's just it," Jason said. "Anything IS possible! Just assume that maybe we're right. Maybe Ulysses Moore came here. Maybe he took the model of the *Nefertiti's Eye* and left the drawing of the *Metis* in exchange. That would explain a lot of things, don't you think? Like why we're here, for example."

"What do you mean . . . why we're here?"

"I mean that I think we were sent here — or lured here — because he needs us to perform a task."

"I don't know," Rick said doubtfully. "That's pretty wild."

"I don't believe that any of this is an accident," Jason said.

"Destiny again?" Rick said.

"Yes, destiny," Jason said with confidence. "We were brought here for a reason. And I think it's to find what Ulysses Moore hid long ago — and return it to Argo Manor!"

"I think you've flipped your lid," Rick said. "But,

well, I have to admit — I don't have a better explanation."

"He sent us here," Jason said. "Ulysses Moore set
up all those clues. He led us to this place."

"Maybe," Rick said. "Except for the fact that
Ulysses Moore is dead."

"That's what you say!" Jason retorted. He thought
back to the noises he had heard coming from the
tower room at Argo Manor. The ghost that wasn't
there.

Maruk walked up between them. "What are you
two whispering about?" she asked.

"I'm sorry, we don't mean to be rude," Jason said.
"Actually, we were just wondering about something. You said that things from all around the world
are brought to the House of Life."

"Yes, that's true."

"Does that mean that, like, anybody can leave
something here?" Jason asked.

"Certainly," Maruk answered. "The House of Life
is known far and wide. All someone has to do is
leave an item with one of the Indexers. They give
their name and pay a small fee."

Rick chimed in, "So if we wanted to find something that was here, and we knew the name of the
person who left it, would that be enough?"

"Maybe we have to find an Indexer," Jason suggested.

"Oh, that is not necessary," said the Great Master Scribe's assistant, who had joined the conversation. "All the names are carefully written down and archived right here, on these very shelves."

Jason and Rick looked at the wooden panels marked with hieroglyphic symbols that, amazingly, they could read as easily as English. One hieroglyph translated in their minds as the letter *M*.

"Moore," Jason said aloud. "Do you think it could be listed here?" he asked Rick.

"I would be happy to assist you," offered the woman.

"Oh no, please, we don't want to take up any more of your time," Rick said. He was reluctant to share any important information. "However, with your permission, we'd be happy to look for it ourselves. We promise to be careful and put everything back in its place."

The woman nodded. "Maruk here can help you. She knows how to find everything in this room," she said. "As for me, I must say good-bye for now. I have my own work to do." The assistant bowed her head, then disappeared the way she had come.

Rick and Jason immediately turned their attention to the shelves again. On each one was a roll of papyrus wrapped in heavy cloth. The rolls contained lists of names, like a modern phone book. But in order to read them all, the boys needed to hold down one end of the papyrus and carefully unroll it until it was spread out on the floor. Each entry, written in meticulous handwriting, contained a name, followed by a brief description of the items left in the Collection. In addition, a short phrase, or code word, was entered beneath the items. According to Maruk, the code indicated the niche in which the item was filed.

"Sounds complicated," Jason groaned.

"Figures," Rick muttered. "Nothing is ever easy. Why couldn't they have written something like, I don't know, 'Storage Box 16,450?'"

"Look at this one," Jason pointed out. "It reads: *The fool searches the world for two cups.*"

"It's a mnemonic device," Maruk explained.

"A new . . . what?" Jason asked.

"Not a new anything. A mnemonic device. A way to help the Indexers remember!" Rick explained. "That's brilliant, absolutely brilliant. They can't remember endless numbers. It's much easier to remember a little story that goes with each item."

"That is correct," Maruk agreed.

"Sure, whatever you say," Jason said, shrugging. They didn't find any mention of Ulysses Moore

until the fourth roll of papyrus. Rick noticed a suspicious dark splotch in the center of it. "Strange," he murmured, and bent over to examine it closely. "Up to now, everything has been written neatly and kept in perfect condition."

Rick leaned close to the splotch, attempting to read the obscured letters. "I think this is it!" he cried, unable to contain his excitement. "But it's been ruined, like someone spilled something on it."

"Or tried to cover it intentionally," Jason hypothesized.

Maruk shook her head. "This is very bad. My father and the Indexers work hard to keep this information safe. And now it looks like someone is trying to sabotage it." She looked at the boys curiously. "Just what is it that you are trying to find?"

But Jason and Rick were too busy trying to decipher the letters that had been covered over to answer. Rick was fairly certain he saw the name *Ulysses Moore.*

Jason studied it, too, and reached the same conclusion. "Everything is all scratched out," he said in disappointment. "The code word is gone. But . . . I think here it says . . . *map.*"

Rick held the papyrus up to the skylight. "Definitely," he determined. "It positively says *map.*"

"You know, if somebody did try to cross off the entry, they didn't do a very good job," Jason noted.

"Maybe they didn't have much time," Rick suggested. "I can't imagine that anyone is allowed to tamper with this stuff."

"That's what I was just trying to tell you," Maruk said, frowning.

Jason smiled at her. "Thanks, Maruk. I promise we'll explain everything. Just — not here."

There was no question that the boys had found a major clue. For here they were, in ancient Egypt, staring at the words: *Ulysses Moore, map.*

Try as they might, those were the only words they could decipher. But it almost didn't matter. They were thrilled. It was more than enough for them to understand that there was something important inside the Collection. Something that they desperately needed to find.

The three kids hurriedly left the room. After walking a short distance, Rick and Jason asked Maruk to stop. They had reached a low-ceilinged room that opened to three different corridors, like spokes on a wheel. Maruk paused before one that was adorned with a statue whose headdress was painted with stars.

"How can you find your way around this place?" Rick asked her. "How come you don't get lost? How is it organized?"

Maruk shrugged, holding the end of her long black braid in her hands. "This is the right way to go, I assure

you," she replied. "It is the Corridor of the Star. Every corridor has its own name. The Indexers understand the system, and they are truly the only ones who do."

"The Indexers," Rick said. "Of course. They use strange codes or story fragments to remember where to find things." He placed a hand on Jason's shoulder. "Like, for example, *After the Emperor, follow the Star.*"

Jason understood immediately. The riddle in the diary. He said, "The niche is under the Star!"

Rick looked at the other two statues in the room. "Like if you wanted to send someone down that hallway, you might say, 'Follow the Priestess until you reach the tower.'"

"Tower?" Jason said.

Rick took a closer look at the statue that stood outside one of the entranceways. "Yeah, tower. What would you call that, Jason? A lighthouse? A tall, skinny building? A pencil?"

"Tower . . . tower," Jason repeated. He rummaged through his bundle, searching for something. "Hold on a minute."

Maruk scratched her head, utterly bewildered. "What are you two talking about now?"

Jason opened up Ulysses Moore's diary and read aloud:

To get your bearings you will need
Good fortune and lucky stars.
Seek out the map in the tower
Under the four wands.

"It's a message," Jason exclaimed. "He gave us the code right here in his diary!"

Maruk peered at the notebook curiously. "What is that?" she asked. "I've never seen anything like that before."

Rick snapped his fingers. "After leaving the map in the Collection," he began, "Ulysses returned to Argo Manor and . . ."

". . . and he wrote the code phrase in his journal so he wouldn't forget it!" Jason finished.

Rick and Jason both let out happy whoops and hugged each other in triumph.

Maruk watched them, a look of amused suspicion on her face. "Why are you here?" she demanded. "What is it that you really want?"

"Maruk, trust us," Jason said, touching her on the arm. "Please, please, trust us."

"Can you take us back to see Pepi and Micerinus?" Rick asked her. "We need to figure out how to interpret this code."

Maruk seemed suddenly distant, distrustful. "Well,

not today," she said. "The Pharaoh will be here for his visit. We can't possibly . . ."

"Maybe we could figure it out ourselves," Jason suggested, too excited to pay attention to Maruk's protest. "*Seek out the map in the tower*," he said aloud. He pointed at the statue. "Well, that looks like a tower to me. Maybe we got lucky. Maybe this is the right corridor!"

Rick shook his head. "Don't you realize how huge this place is? There's no way we just happily stumbled upon the right corridor."

But Jason wasn't listening. He headed into the Corridor of the Priestess, calling back over his shoulder, "I'll be right back, just chill out."

Maruk looked at Rick questioningly. "Chill . . . out?"

"No way," Rick called back, hurrying after Jason. "Not again. I'm not going to let you disappear like your sister did."

"Sister?" Maruk asked, trotting along behind them.

In the Corridor of the Priestess, Rick and Jason started to carefully examine and count the symbols marked on each individual niche. There were two rows of niches on each side: On one side, the lower row was marked by the symbol of a goblet and the upper one with a sword. On the opposite side of the corridor, they were marked with coins and wands.

"Wands!" Rick cried out. "We've got to find the one with four wands!"

It wasn't difficult. All they had to do was continue on until they found the fourth niche on the right-hand side.

"Rats! It's empty," Jason huffed, looking into the fourth cubby.

"Rats?" Maruk said fearfully, searching the floor.

"No, not real rats," Jason explained, laughing. "I mean rats, like, um, bad news."

Maruk stared at him blankly. "You seem very nice," she finally said. "But I have no idea what you are talking about most of the time."

"Don't worry," Jason reassured her, "neither do I."

Rick joined them, frowning into the empty niche. "Yeah, I guess it would've been too easy. And where's the fun in that?" He slumped to the floor, disappointed.

Jason continued farther down the corridor, counting out loud, "Five wands, six, seven, eight, nine, ten wands, and, what? Oh no!" he said, stopping suddenly.

"More rats?" wondered Maruk.

"Worse," Jason called back. "It's a boy leaning on a wand."

"What?!" Rick was on his feet again, hurrying to reach Jason.

"I figured I'd find eleven wands," Jason explained. "You know, because eleven follows ten and everything."

"Wow, you really are a math whiz," Rick noted.

Jason let that remark pass without comment. "But instead of eleven wands, here's a symbol of a boy leaning against a wand."

Rick walked farther on, disappearing around the corner of the corridor.

Maruk followed them, drawn by her own curiosity. "I told you before. Nobody can understand any of this except the Indexers."

"Here's one of a girl holding a wand!" Rick called out. "And then a woman, and then a bearded man! And then the corridor comes to an end."

Rick rejoined Jason and Maruk. He was bursting with excitement. "I've got it!" he announced. "I know why there are fifty-six niches in each corridor!"

"Okaaay," Jason said. "Clue me in, Sherlock."

Rick pointed to the niches. "Think of a deck of cards, Jason. It goes from one — the aces — to ten, and then you have the face cards — jack, queen, and king. Just like you do here! The wands go from one to ten, then the boy, the girl, the woman, and the bearded man! The other symbols have a boy, a girl, a woman, and a man, too. I checked."

Jason frowned. "But playing cards have only three

face cards, not four." He looked again at the different rows of niches. "But there are goblets instead of hearts, swords instead of spades, wands instead of clubs, and, um, coins instead of diamonds. So it's almost the same, but not quite. Cool, very cool!"

Rick turned to Maruk. "So that's it? That's the big secret code? A deck of cards?"

Maruk looked at him blankly. "Hearts and diamonds? I don't understand, Rick."

"You mean to tell me you've never played cards before?" Rick said. But even as he said it, he knew the answer. Of course she hadn't. They were in ancient Egypt, not at the World Championship of Poker.

Maruk shook her head. "We play senet, or astragals, mostly."

Rick and Jason exchanged a clueless look. The three of them slowly walked back into the room from which they had come.

"It makes sense, though," Rick said. "Maruk has never played cards because they haven't been invented yet."

"Right," Jason said. "It's like expecting her to know about playing Madden Football on PlayStation."

"Yeah, sort of," Rick said. "By the way, Jason — you are a real freak sometimes, you know that?"

Jason gave Rick a playful slap on the side of the head.

"I think both of you are quite strange," Maruk
commented.

Rick and Jason looked at her, then at each other,
and burst out laughing. But a few seconds later,
Rick was back to business. "Okay, the niches are
numbered like a deck of cards — even though the
Egyptians don't even know about playing cards. A
nice little riddle right there, I'd say."

He paused before the entrance to the Corridor of
the Priestess, puzzling over the statue that guarded
it. Rick scratched his head, still trying to work everything out logically.

"The problem remains," he continued, "even if
we've figured out that the niches are numbered like
cards, how do the statues fit in with all of this?"

"The statues give us the names of the corridors,"
Jason said. "Right?"

At that moment, the silence was shattered by the
blaring of trumpets.

"Quickly!" cried Maruk, grabbing her friends'
sleeves. "The trumpets!"

"What's going on?" Jason shouted over the din.

"We must go now," Maruk pleaded. "When the
trumpets sound, everyone must leave the Collection
immediately!"

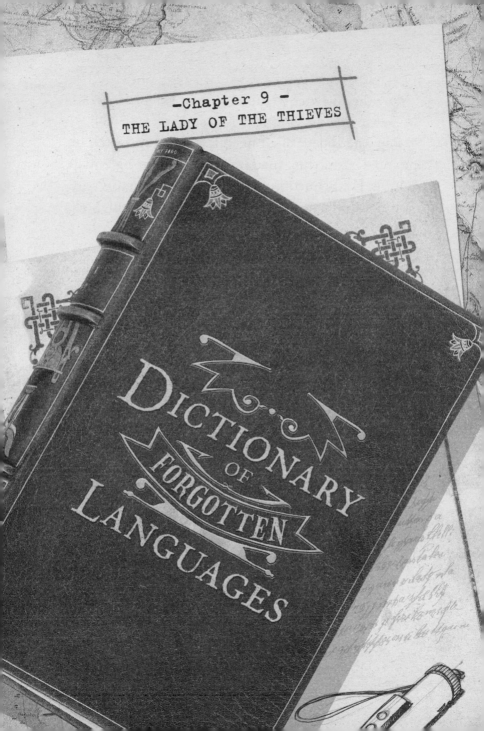

DICTIONARY
OF
FORGOTTEN
LANGUAGES

At the entrance to the House of Life, two people were having a loud disagreement.

Pepi the Indexer had been left alone to watch his post. "That is true, madam. It may only be a map, but, as I explained before . . ." Pepi smiled wanly, hoping desperately that Micerinus would soon return.

"It is located in this building, isn't that correct? Am I right or am I wrong?" badgered the woman who stood before the mild Indexer. Her tone was rude, condescending, and seething with impatience.

"Oh, naturally, I am sure it is located in the Collection as you say," Pepi stammered. "The problem, however, is that, er, Rule Number . . ."

"Not again with the rules!" the woman screeched.

"But rules are rules," Pepi replied hopefully. Sweat began to form on his upper lip. "Your name again, madam?"

"Newton," the woman stated. "Oblivia Newton." She towered threateningly over Pepi as he hunched behind a small desk. Oblivia reached down and pinned Pepi's hand to the desktop.

The Indexer's eyes opened wide. He tried to pull back his hand subtly, but it was no use. His fingers were trapped in the woman's grasp.

"You see," Pepi tried to explain, "there are regulations that must be followed. At this moment — by the way, you are hurting my pinkie ever so slightly — um, it is not possible to . . ."

"Go in?" the woman said.

"Yes! Exactly!" exclaimed a relieved Pepi. "The Pharaoh is in town, you realize. We have orders to suspend all consultation services until the Divine Ruler has finished visiting the Collection. Surely you understand?"

"No, *you* don't seem to understand the seriousness of my request," Oblivia said, leaning close to the man. Her nails dug deeper into the top of his flabby hand.

"You are hurting me just a little," Pepi whimpered.

The woman released his hand. "Are you telling me that my entire journey here was for nothing? That I came all this way just to hear a mere minion tell me that it is not possible to go inside? Your petty rules and regulations make me ill."

The woman placed a bag of coins on the table. She pushed them toward Pepi.

"Oh please, no," the Indexer stammered. "I cannot accept a br — that is, your gift," he said. "Rule Number Seventeen strictly forbids it. Please, madam, I beg you. I will be only too happy to accommodate your wishes on another day."

Oblivia Newton's eyes became daggers. "I must get in," she insisted. "It is urgent. I must have that map!"

"I . . . I am not . . . authorized," Pepi tried to explain. "The rules are very clear. No one is allowed to enter."

"Until when?"

"Until, as I have tried to explain, the young Pharaoh has completed his visit," Pepi said.

Oblivia tried a different tactic. Her voice softened. She smiled sweetly. "I simply need a little look, just a quick peek," the woman cooed. She grasped the feather sticking up out of Pepi's headdress and smoothed it back over his head. "You will not regret this act of kindness."

Pepi was by now drenched in sweat, a stammering mess of a man. "I suppose that . . . perhaps if . . ."

A blast of trumpets suddenly echoed through the room, momentarily silencing the vast crowd.

Pepi leaned back in his chair as if breaking away from an enchantment. His heart leaped when he spotted Micerinus making his way toward them. The sight of his colleague gave Pepi the strength he needed. "I am sorry, madam, but that is my final word. You cannot enter. It is not permitted!"

Pepi folded his arms defiantly.

Oblivia Newton stood still, holding a single feather in her hand. She threw it to ground and mashed it with the heel of her sandal. More trumpets blared.

All visitors in the House of Life were being ushered outside.

"There must be a way inside," she hissed. "Oblivia Newton does not give up so easily." But what could she do? If Manfred were here, he could have swiftly dealt with this whimpering little man. But Oblivia could not afford to wait.

A low, mirthless laugh came to her ears. Oblivia turned to see a young man, just a teenage boy, really. He was leaning against a column, laughing — laughing at her.

"Is something funny?" she snarled.

The young man's expression did not change. He stood and grinned, dark eyes twinkling. He pushed himself away from the column with calculated slowness and, ignoring the crowd of people around them, walked directly to her.

"You wish to find a way inside the Collection," he said in a low tone.

Oblivia nodded. "Yes, very much."

"There might be a way," the boy said. "I heard you tell the Indexer that you were seeking a map."

"Possibly," said Oblivia, as she sized up the boy. His clothes were dirty and wrinkled. He looked thin, underfed. A street urchin, she decided. Probably cunning and clever. Perhaps even dangerous.

And very likely to be only too happy to break the rules for a price.

"I know a place in the city," the boy said. "A shop where they sell many rare maps."

Oblivia scoffed. "I highly doubt that your shop has the map that I seek. There is only one copy." She pointed down the corridors of the House of Life. "And unfortunately for me, it is hidden in there."

Oblivia placed a hand on the urchin's chest and pushed him gently to the side. "Now run along and do whatever it is that you do," she said. "I have more important matters to attend to."

The young man let her pass, breathing in her heavy perfume. "In that case," he called after her, "we will have to sneak in and look for it ourselves."

Oblivia sized him up with a stare.

The boy held a hand above his head and nodded as if giving a signal.

Suddenly, around the great central pit, there was a disturbance amongst the crowd — a fight between several dirty-faced boys. There was wild shouting, pushing, and punches thrown. A group of guards hurried off to secure the area.

"Now is our chance," said the boy, eyes twinkling mischievously.

Oblivia smiled. "I like your style," she purred.

"You'll like it even more," he said, "after you pay me."

Oblivia locked her arm around his elbow. "Oh you will be rewarded handsomely, young man. You and I will get along very well. But first, lead the way."

At Maruk's urging, Jason and Rick started running. They reached a stairway that spiraled down into an enormous empty corridor. They headed down a dark passageway, then ran into a large room with a ceiling decorated with stars.

More trumpets sounded, making their hearts pound.

All of a sudden, Rick stopped in his tracks.

"Come on!" urged Maruk. "We must leave now! The Pharaoh is arriving!"

"Wait, please!" Rick pleaded. "I need to think for a minute." He stared up at the starry ceiling. Then he dropped his bundle to the floor and pulled out the *Dictionary of Forgotten Languages*.

Jason rushed back to Rick, panting. "What are you doing? You heard Maruk. The guards will find us!"

"I have to look up something," Rick insisted. "Give me a couple of minutes, that's all I'm asking."

Jason sighed, then turned to Maruk. "I have a confession," he told her. "But you have to promise that you will keep it a secret."

Maruk nodded, transfixed by his sudden earnestness.

"We haven't been entirely truthful," Jason confessed. "We didn't come here with the fleet."

Maruk nodded and smiled slightly. "I know," she said.

Meanwhile, Rick frantically leafed through the pages of the dictionary. He looked up to study his surroundings. There were two statues nearby. One was of a man hanging upside down from a tree. The other was of a dead man. Rick turned to the dictionary's index. He started under the heading "Languages of Ancient Egypt."

"You knew?" Jason said to Maruk.

"Yes, I knew," she replied. "You and Rick came from far away, I realize that. But you did not come with the fleet. I have seen many distant travelers, but I have never met anyone like you before."

"I'm sorry that we lied to you," Jason said. "We told you we came here with the fleet because otherwise you never would have believed us." He glanced back at Rick, trying to buy his friend a few more minutes' time. "It was almost true, kind of," Jason explained. "We did come here on a ship. And the truth is, Maruk, we don't even know exactly how we got here, or why. But we need you to help us. I'm just asking you . . . no, I'm begging you . . . to please trust us for a little while longer."

Maruk hesitated, glancing toward Rick. "I don't know if I *can* trust you," she said. "But you came to me in my hour of need. I was hurt and fallen. I owe both of you a debt of gratitude."

"Thank you," Jason said. "But we're the ones who owe you."

Maruk glanced again at Rick, a puzzled look on her face. "What is Rick doing?"

"It's a book," Jason said. "It contains writing, like your scrolls, but in a different form."

Rick did not even bother to look up at them. "I'm trying to figure out how the code to the Collection works," he told Maruk. "We need to find a map."

Maruk shook her head vigorously. "But you cannot look for it now! We have to leave, or the guards will drag us away. And my father will be very, very angry and embarrassed."

"If we leave now," Rick stated, "we may never have the chance to come back again. It's now or never."

"But why not?" Maruk protested. "We can come back tomorrow. There are many days ahead."

Jason shook his head gently. "Rick is right, Maruk. We have lingered too long in your world already. My sister is already home. We have to get back to her. But first, there is one task we must complete."

"A task?" Maruk said. "What is it?"

Rick looked up from his book and gave a short, bitter laugh. "Well, we're not exactly sure."

Maruk's curiosity began to overpower her fear of the guards. "Where are you from? Did someone send you here?"

Jason lifted his hands in frustration. "We don't know, Maruk," he said. "Believe me, I wish I could tell you more. All we have is a clue. One small clue that we discovered in your father's office. Do you remember the name we were looking for in the scrolls? He is . . . a friend," Jason said.

The walls of the House of Life echoed with yet another blast of trumpets.

Maruk grabbed Jason's hand. She looked at him with pleading, innocent eyes. "I do trust you, Jason. But now you must trust me. If we stay here, we will be in serious trouble. It is forbidden to disregard the call of the Royal Guard."

But she was interrupted by a gasp from Rick.

"I think I found something!" he exclaimed.

EGYPTE

15

LE CAIRE ... CONGRÈS INTERNATIONAL DE NAVIGATION

YSSES MOORE
RGO MANOR
MORE COVE 74820
SALTON CLIFF
WALL (UK)

Covenant

Ancient Egyptian tarot
cards! I found them tucked
inside Ulysses Moore's journal.

Jason knelt at Rick's side. The book was open to a chart of drawings numbered from zero to twenty-two.

"Tarot cards," Rick murmured. "Why didn't I think of that before?"

The dictionary explained that tarot cards were the most ancient playing cards in the world, and that all modern cards were derived from them. Some believed that tarot cards depicted the Tablets of Knowledge through which the Egyptian god Thoth had taught man the secrets of writing, arithmetic, music, and games. For this reason, the different parts of the deck were called Arcana, or things that are arcane, mysterious, puzzling.

Rick read aloud, hungry to learn more: "*A deck of Tarot cards is divided into fifty-six Minor Arcana cards and twenty-two Major Arcana cards. The fifty-six Minor Arcana cards are divided into four suits: cups, coins, swords, and wands.*" Rick looked up at Maruk and Jason and beamed. "Just like the niches in the corridors!"

"Listen to this," Jason said. He read aloud: "*The Major Arcana consist of twenty-two cards depicting figures with unknown meanings.*"

Maruk nodded enthusiastically. "Finally," she said, "here's something I know about." She pointed to the various statues in the room. "Card number twenty-one represents the World. Number twelve," she said, pointing to the nearest statue, "the Hanged Man. Major Arcana card number thirteen . . ." she said, turning and pointing to the statue behind her, "represents Death!"

"So that's why number thirteen brings bad luck," Jason mused. "After all, you have to admit that being dead is pretty unlucky."

He reached for Ulysses Moore's diary and stared at the coded message:

To get your bearings you will need
Good fortune and lucky stars.
Seek out the map in the tower
Under the four wands.

Maruk touched Jason on the shoulder. "We must leave here, or everything we've learned will be wasted. The guards," she whispered.

Jason shot a look at Rick, who didn't budge. He seemed lost in thought. "Micerinus said that the Collection was divided into twenty-two sections, each with twenty-two rooms, and each of those with twenty-two corridors," Rick reminded them. "Twenty-two. That's the same number as the Major Arcana cards!"

Maruk began pacing nervously.

"One more minute, Maruk," Jason pleaded. "If we want to find the map of the four wands, then four wands must be the symbol of the niche. And we know that the map is found in the tower. . . ."

"*The Tower*," Rick read from the dictionary, "*Major Arcana card number sixteen.* Ulysses Moore's code says that to find it, we will need good fortune and lucky stars."

He snapped the book shut and slowly lifted his chin toward the ceiling. It was painted to resemble a starry night sky.

"Okay," he said. "Fortune is card number ten. The Star is card seventeen. Don't you get it, Jason? When we went into the Corridor of the Priestess, it was the wrong way."

"My head is beginning to hurt," Jason groaned.

"Let me explain it," Rick offered.

"No. Don't explain anything or my head will explode," Jason protested. "As long as *you* understand it, that's good enough for me."

Rick looked at Maruk. "All we've got to do is figure out where we are. Do you know? Can you help us, please?"

"We are in the section of Good Fortune," she replied.

"Great, Good Fortune — that sure beats Death,

any day of the week!" Jason cried. "So now where do we go?"

Rick walked toward the corridor guarded by the figure of Death, Major Arcana card number thirteen.

"If this is the Room of the Star, then we're really close now," he determined. "We've got to find the Corridor of the Tower, that is, we've got to go . . ."

". . . that way," Maruk said, pointing down a long hallway. "But let's hurry. Anything is better than standing around here talking, waiting for the guards to arrest us."

"Oh, thank you, Maruk — you are awesome!" Jason said. Without thinking, he hugged her.

Maruk blushed deeply. "I will help you," she said. "But only until we hear the trumpets call again. After that, I must leave you."

They started to run. The sound of their sandals on the pavement echoed against the building's tiled floor and stone walls.

Guided by Maruk, they reached a corridor that was guarded by the statue of a man who looked like an angel. The next statue depicted a winged demon. Finally, they came to the statue of the Tower.

Jason surged to the front excitedly. He counted the niches as he ran — one wand, two wands, three wands. "Here it is!" he cried.

He had stopped before two large niches. The lower one was of the four coins, and it was filled with papyruses and scrolls. The niche of the four wands was slightly above eye level. Its opening was covered with a spider's web.

Rick pulled out the last candle stub from their bundle of supplies. Maruk watched in awe as he struck a match, lit the candle, and handed it to Jason. "You look!" he told his friend. "I'll boost you up."

Rick clasped his hands together for Jason to step into. He lifted Jason up just high enough to look inside the niche of the four wands.

"Careful, Jason," Maruk whispered as he leaned forward into the niche, holding up the candle in front of him.

"Hurry up," Rick said, grunting from the effort. "I can't hold you much longer."

At this, Maruk stepped forward to help steady Jason.

"I don't see anything," Jason said.

The niche seemed totally empty. Disappointed, Jason was just about to ask his friends to lower him down when he spotted a small sheet of papyrus that had been shoved into the corner, way in the back. He set down the candle stub, reached out and snatched the paper with his fingertips. "Bingo!" he exclaimed.

At that moment, Maruk whispered tensely, "Someone's coming!" Panicked, she stepped away from the boys. As she did, Rick staggered, and Jason tumbled down on top of him. He clutched the papyrus in his hand. Maruk ran down the corridor and disappeared from view. Jason and Rick scrambled up from the floor, slightly dazed. They heard two sets of footsteps approaching.

Rick pointed at the lower niche, the one of the Four Coins. "Quick! Hide in there!"

The boys slipped inside the large niche, ducking behind the rolls of papyrus. They closed their eyes. Held their breath. And listened as the sound of footsteps echoed closer and closer.

"How much longer is this going to take?" Oblivia Newton muttered. She walked beside the young urchin along yet another corridor, which looked identical to all the others before it.

"You are an impatient woman," the boy noted with a trace of scorn. "And far too noisy. If you wish to find the map, you must keep your mouth shut."

Oblivia bristled at the boy's impertinence. "Hasn't anyone taught you any manners?"

The boy stopped right in the middle of a high-walled room. He looked up. The ceiling was dotted with stars. He turned to Oblivia. "Listen to me carefully," he said harshly. "If someone had taught me manners, if I had a mother or a father who I remembered, then I would not have ended up here, helping you sneak through these corridors to steal a map."

Oblivia glared at the young man. Ever since they'd first entered the Collection rooms, walking up and down endless hallways, the boy had done nothing but treat her rudely. In fact, he acted as if he were herding a cow!

"No, you listen to *me*," Oblivia snarled. "I paid you handsomely. I refuse to be treated this way."

The boy laughed quietly. "You refuse? What will you do to me? Or better yet, consider what you would do if I abandoned you here in this maze."

Oblivia gritted her teeth.

The boy continued, speaking in a low whisper. "I did not agree to bring you here just to get caught by the Pharaoh's guards. If you don't keep quiet, they *will* find us. And I promise you that being left alone to rot in a dark cell, shared by dozens of red-eyed rats, is not how you would like to grow old."

Oblivia shivered involuntarily. She did not care for rats.

"I have no intention of getting caught," she replied.

"Good, then we understand each other," the boy said. "Now follow me. We are almost there."

They turned into the Corridor of the Tower and paced along it until they reached the niche marked by the four wands.

"This is it," the young man announced.

Oblivia shoved him aside and bent down, peering into the lower niche, which was filled with papyrus.

"Not that one," the boy said. "The one above it."

Oblivia eagerly rose up on tiptoes, stretching to see inside the niche. "At last!" she cried with glee. "I've finally beaten you, Ulysses Moore!"

At that moment, she thought she heard a muffled gasp. "Did you say something?" she asked the boy.

"Not a word," he replied. "Quickly, woman. Take what you came for. We must be on our way. This place is crawling with guards."

Again Oblivia rose on her tiptoes. She murmured, "Patience, you skittery child. Let me enjoy the moment. I've waited so many years for it."

Hiding in the niche below, Jason and Rick listened as she flicked a lighter to see inside. For a long moment, there was silence. Then —

"It cannot be," Oblivia cried in disbelief. "It's empty — EMPTY!"

"*Shhh*," the boy said, bringing a finger to his lips.

Oblivia, true to her name, was oblivious to his

request. "There is nothing here, you thief!" Oblivia cried, turning on the young man. "Nothing but this — a candle stub!"

"You must be quiet," the young man urged her. "The Pharaoh's guards could be near."

Oblivia's face turned crimson red. It was all she could do to contain the burning anger growing inside her.

"I'm leaving," her guide hissed.

But Oblivia grabbed him by the arm. "Oh no, you don't!" she snapped. "What are you trying to pull? This is a trick, a street urchin's game. You've deliberately led me to the wrong place, haven't you?"

The boy pulled his arm away. "Do not touch me, woman," he snarled. "I have followed your instructions perfectly. This is exactly where you told me to go."

"Then why isn't it here?!" Oblivia cried. "Who else could have taken the secret map of Kilmore Cove?"

Jason jabbed Rick in the ribs.

"That is none of my concern," the young man growled. "I held up my end of the bargain. I have acted with honor. The rest is for you to worry about."

Oblivia Newton clenched her fists. Perhaps it was true. Perhaps this was the right niche. Perhaps someone else had arrived here before her ... an enemy bent on thwarting her plans.

Muffled footsteps reached their ears — the clatter of soldiers approaching.

"They have heard us. I know another way out. Come, quickly!" the boy whispered tensely.

Oblivia nodded. She felt the candle stub in her hand. Strange, to find one here in Egypt, in an empty niche. "Get us out of here," she demanded.

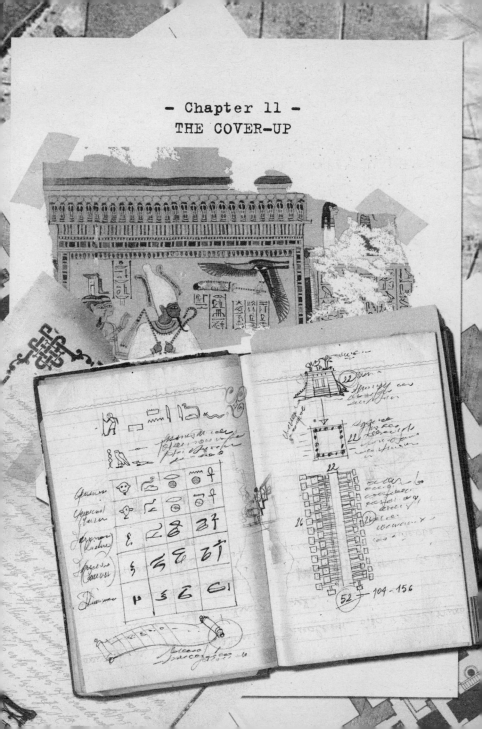

The Pharaoh's guards came in haste. They probed the corridor with the tips of their spears, talking casually amongst themselves. After a few moments, they moved on. The sound of their footsteps soon faded away.

Jason and Rick stayed frozen in silence, not daring to move or utter a sound. Only after what felt like hours did they push aside the papyruses and emerge from their hiding place.

The corridor was empty.

"Maruk?" Jason called in a stage whisper.

"Quiet," Rick warned. "Let's hope she escaped."

"You heard it all?" Jason asked Rick.

"Every word," he answered. "Oblivia Newton is here, searching for the map." He sniffed the air, recognizing Oblivia's heavy perfume. He had met her only once before, when her car had nearly run him off the road to Argo Manor, but the scent was unforgettable.

Jason showed his friend the strip of papyrus he had found in the niche. "Too bad," he said with a smile, "we beat her to it."

But the papyrus was not a map. Instead, it contained a short message written with the same symbols used in the notes they had found in the box in the side of the cliff and the package they had recovered with the help of Ms. Calypso — the clues that had led them to the grotto and the *Metis*.

"Another puzzle," Rick groaned unhappily.

Jason nodded. "The writing is the same as the others," he noted. "Hieroglyphs from the Phaistos Disk."

"And the search goes on," Rick said. There was disappointment in his voice.

"We can't translate it now," Jason said. "The guards could return any minute. We've got to find a way out of here." He looked around, turning in a full circle. "Um, Rick? Got any bright ideas?"

"I always do," Rick replied, leading the way out of the corridor.

"So, who is Oblivia Newton, exactly?" Jason asked his friend as they walked.

"I don't really know for sure," Rick replied. "I've

only met her once, on the road to your house. I saw her arguing with Nestor. She travels with a big goon named Manfred." Rick thought for a moment. "Gwendaline would know," he decided.

"Gwendaline?"

"Yes, the hairdresser in Kilmore Cove," Rick answered. "She's the town gossip. My mom says that if a fly landed in Kilmore Cove, Gwendaline would know about it."

"I still can't get over it," Jason mused. "Oblivia Newton . . . in Egypt. Could she have traveled here on the *Metis*, too?"

They turned down another corridor dominated by the statue of a winged demon. "I don't know, but you heard what she said," Rick remarked. "'I've finally beaten you, Ulysses Moore!'"

Jason nodded ruefully. "Yes, and I almost got us caught when I gasped," he admitted. "But at least we're learning more and more. Now we know that Oblivia hates the old owner of Argo Manor. What was she arguing about with Nestor?"

"I didn't catch most of the words," Rick said. "They both seemed really angry. I thought it was about Argo Manor."

"Do you think that Oblivia knows about the door, the grotto, and the ship?" Jason wondered.

Rick shrugged. "Possibly," he remarked. "After

all, she got here somehow — and I doubt she took a bus."

As Jason walked, a word suddenly flashed in his mind: *Cover-up*. His mind raced through a series of images: the old door covered with scratches and burn marks, hidden behind a heavy armoire. The postal package that had not been claimed. The underground passageway that had caved in and was blocked. The diary in which the captain of the *Metis* said it would be his last voyage.

"It's all been covered up!" he cried out. "Covered up or erased. Think about it, Rick! The wall that sealed off the corridor, the register entry scratched out, the niche emptied. Everything has been hidden from us! It's like someone is trying to prevent us from discovering the truth."

"Or to prevent Oblivia Newton from discovering it," Rick replied grimly.

Back in Cleopatra Biggles's sitting room, Manfred let out a lazy yawn. He tossed a dull ladies' magazine onto the coffee table and stretched his legs.

Miss Biggles lay sleeping heavily on the sofa, her mouth open wide, dead to the world.

Manfred got up and rummaged around in the

kitchen. All he found in the fridge were vegetables and wafer cookies. He munched on a few cookies out of boredom.

Oblivia's crushing insults echoed in his mind again and again:

"*Must I tell you everything?*"

"*Do I have to explain everything to you?*"

"*Can't you figure out the simplest things for yourself?*"

The words troubled him, angered him, and, finally, spurred him to action.

"I have ideas," he grumbled. "You'll see, Oblivia. I can figure things out. I'm not as dumb as you think."

He looked out the window. The storm still raged. The street was empty. The car was parked by the curb. Manfred grabbed his raincoat, slipped it on, opened the door, and walked out.

"You'll be proud of me, Oblivia Newton," Manfred muttered to himself as he pulled the car from the curb. "Just wait till you see what I can do."

He was headed to Argo Manor.

Inside the old house, Julia gazed out the large windows of the portico. She could not sleep. In truth, she had been awakened by nightmares. Nestor stood beside her silently. Together they looked out at the driving rain. A beacon from the lighthouse sliced through the darkness, lending the night an eerie quality.

"Does the lighthouse go on every night?" Julia asked the caretaker.

"No, only during storms," Nestor answered. He sighed deeply, then turned and went into the kitchen.

Julia leaned against the statue of the fisherwoman, lost in thought. A noise drew her to the foot of the stairs. She paused, goose bumps rising on her arms. Something was moving upstairs.

"Nestor?" she called in a whisper.

Julia heard another noise. She held on to the iron handrail and climbed the first step.

"Nestor? Is that you?"

Cautiously, step by step, Julia climbed the stairs. From the top, she could see through a small window that overlooked the front courtyard and gardens.

A broad beam of light moved across the yard. The lighthouse? No, that wasn't it. Then she heard the unmistakable hum of a car engine. A black car had pulled into the courtyard of Argo Manor.

Julia bolted down the stairs. "Nestor!" she shouted. "Nestor!"

- Chapter 12 -
REUNION

I think this is a photo of
Manfred—he certainly
matches the kids' description.

The sound of trumpets, followed by thunderous applause, stopped Rick and Jason in their tracks. They were close, very close, to an exit.

Jason peeked cautiously around the corner. He saw an ocher room, all buttery yellow, with an archway window that overlooked a vast, parklike area. The room was abandoned. The applause had come from just beyond the archway.

The two boys peered through the window. A festive crowd filled the grounds on both sides of the main thoroughfare. An open chariot drawn by two black horses was moving slowly down the avenue, under a spectacular shower of flower petals.

"It's the Pharaoh! Tutankhamen!" Jason cried when he saw the child Pharaoh inside the chariot.

Tutankhamen waved to the delighted crowd with broad, sweeping gestures. An elegant man with a thick white beard held the reins as the chariot wound down the road.

The man's face looked strangely familiar. "Could that be Maruk's father?" Rick wondered aloud. He was a possible link to Argo Manor. For Rick felt certain, given the clues they had already found, that somehow the Great Master Scribe was connected to Ulysses Moore.

Jason watched the scene with excitement. Oh,

what he would have given to be down below in the garden, along with the teeming crowd, staring into the eyes of the Pharaoh!

"We'd better keep moving," Rick said, breaking into Jason's reverie. "It isn't safe here."

"Psssst!" came a voice. "Jason, Rick! I'm down here!" Maruk's head popped out from a niche at their feet.

"Maruk!" cried Jason. "How did you get here?"

Their friend smiled up at them brightly. She climbed out of the niche and got to her feet. "I've been hiding here and there, trying to avoid the guards — and hoping to find you again. Please," she said. "We must go."

"I won't argue with that," said Rick.

Maruk led them down a steep staircase. "While I was hiding, I heard someone else pass. Other people trying to hide from the guards."

Rick and Jason exchanged a look. "A woman and a teenage boy — a thief?" Jason asked.

Maruk's eyes widened. "Yes! Did you hear them, too?"

"We sure did," said Rick grimly. "Did you hear them speak? Did they say anything important?"

"Oh yes," Maruk answered. "The woman was very angry. The boy said that they should go to the Shop of Long-Lost Maps."

"Wow! Great detective work, Maruk," Jason exclaimed. "Can you take us there?"

Maruk nodded. In a moment, they had slipped into the garden and were milling along the edge of the crowd. Maruk led them to a quiet street lined with small palm trees. There they paused for a moment to examine the sheet of papyrus they'd discovered inside the niche. With the help of the dictionary, Rick and Jason quickly translated its message:

I have moved the map to a safe place:
The room that isn't there.

"Oh great," Rick moaned. "Just terrific. Now we have to find a room that doesn't exist."

"This clue will not help you very much," Maruk commented. "I believe that your friend is playing a joke."

"Why do you think that?" asked Jason.

"He says he has hidden your map in the Room That Isn't There. That means he has destroyed it."

"I don't get it," Jason said.

"It's a legend," Maruk explained. "A fable. Putting something in the Room That Isn't There means throwing it away, putting it in a place that doesn't exist. Destroying it."

"Are you sure?" Rick asked. "It doesn't seem consistent with everything we've learned so far. Every clue has led us to something."

"Well, after today, I will never be sure of anything again!" Maruk said with a shy smile. "But it is like 'The Ballad of Two Lovers,' who get lost and wander around hoping to find each other again. They, too, are lost in a room that doesn't exist."

Jason rubbed his forehead. "Here comes that old headache again," he grumbled.

Rick was adamant. "I don't believe it," he said. "Ulysses said that he put the map in a safe place — he doesn't say that he destroyed it."

"But that is the safest place of all," Maruk countered. "The map is safe. I believe that is what your friend, this Ulysses, was trying to tell you."

"I refuse to believe that," Rick said. "There must be a map of Kilmore Cove hidden here in Egypt. And judging from what we just saw in the corridor with Oblivia Newton, the map must be very, very important."

Jason agreed with his friend. "I'm sorry, Maruk. I can't stop believing that the map still exists . . . somewhere. Too many strange things have brought us down this path. We can't give up now. That map

might explain the mystery of the door in Argo Manor. No," he said resolutely, "we've got to find the Room That Isn't There — before Oblivia Newton beats us to it!"

"Well, sure," Rick said. "That's easy to say. But where do we start looking?"

"You are both crazy!" Maruk said. "That is an impossible task, a job for a fool. You might as well search for a single grain of sand in the desert!"

"I guess we better get started then," Jason said to Rick. "We don't have all day."

"Well, we do have one clue," Rick added. He turned to Maruk. "Tell us what you know about the Shop of Long-Lost Maps."

"Nestor?!" Julia whispered hoarsely.

No answer.

Acting on instinct, Julia hid behind the statue of the fisherwoman. She was grateful for the room's darkness. She could see the long, dark car parked outside on the gravel driveway. When the car door opened, the light inside flashed on. Julia gave a start when she saw a menacing man behind the wheel. He looked large and dangerous.

In that instant, Julia knew at once that this was not a social visit, but one that held great peril.

The man strode toward the front door. Julia heard him as he tried the doorknob. She felt a wave of relief as she realized that it was locked.

His shadow passed by the window as he walked around to the back of the house. He disappeared from sight, swallowed up by the darkness.

A rough hand closed around Julia's arm. She was pulled up from where she crouched on the floor.

"Shhh," whispered Nestor. "Stay quiet. Let's hope he goes away."

"But . . . who . . . ?"

"*Shhh,*" Nestor breathed. "Not a sound."

Gently, he pulled her back into the shadows, pausing at the bottom of the stairs. There was a flash of lightning, followed by thunder. The large intruder suddenly appeared outside the window. Nestor's hand clamped over Julia's mouth, stifling her startled cry.

The stranger pressed his face up to the window. He peered inside.

"He can't see us," Nestor whispered to Julia. "We are hidden in the darkness. The doors and windows are all secure, I've made sure of that."

"But what if . . . ?"

"He cannot enter," Nestor promised. "The house is sealed, the glass is shatterproof."

Julia raised her eyebrows. *Shatterproof?*

The intruder began to check the perimeter of the house methodically — every door, every window.

"The kitchen door?" Julia whispered.

"Locked," Nestor whispered.

"The window in the stone room!" Julia said with alarm. "You opened it earlier, when I felt faint."

Nestor was silent for a moment. "Stay right here," he warned at last, then disappeared into the darkness.

Julia stood paralyzed with fear, her heart pounding, as she waited for Nestor to return. She could hear the wind outside, the rattling of windows.

The intruder was at the portico now, rattling each of the four doors in turn.

"Locked, locked, locked," Julia murmured to herself as if in prayer.

He reached the fourth door, his hand on the doorknob.

Julia's eyes widened in fright.

The handle moved. The door was unlocked.

Without hesitation, Julia leaped out of the shadows. "No!" she screamed, charging toward the door, both arms raised.

Manfred paused with the door only slightly ajar.

He was startled to discover that someone was inside; he had assumed that everyone was upstairs, asleep.

Julia reached the door and threw her body against it, slamming it shut.

The man staggered back from the blow. He bent down, cradling his nose in his hands.

Julia turned the lock. "Nestor!" she screamed.

"Julia?! Are you all right?" Nestor called out. He came running to her side.

Julia pointed outside the glass door, unable to find the words. And there was Manfred, still bent over in obvious pain. Blood trickled through his fingers. He stared at Julia through the glass door. "You broke my nose!" he howled.

Enraged, he flung his body against the glass door. *BOOM!*

Julia clutched at Nestor's shirt. But the door held firm.

Manfred screamed like a madman. "I'll destroy you!" he cried. "I'll tear down this house brick by brick! Nothing can stop me."

"He will not succeed," Nestor whispered into Julia's ear. "I will protect you. Trust me."

Again and again Manfred threw himself against the door, his frustration mounting with each blow. His screams were filled with fury.

The beacon from the lighthouse swept slowly across the garden, washing the bloodstained brute in light.

"Who is he?" Julia asked Nestor. "What does he want?"

"I gather," Nestor said with uncanny calm, "that he wants to get out of the rain."

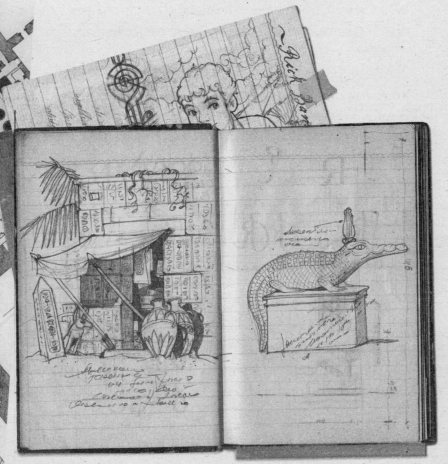

*Another sketch from Ulysses's notebook I believe this
is the shop of Long-Lost Maps.*

J ason, Rick, and Maruk strode swiftly down the avenue lined with sphinxes. All the while, Maruk peppered the boys with questions. How did they come to the Land of Punt? Where did they live? What was it like in their homeland? Her curiosity was overwhelming — she wanted to learn everything.

And so Jason told her every detail, from the beginning. In telling it, he could not help but realize that it must sound like a dream, a wild fantasy beyond imagining. There was no way that Maruk could ever truly grasp the world he described to her, no matter how patiently he tried.

He spoke of Julia, and how she had disappeared back through the door to time. He told her about Argo Manor and Ulysses Moore.

Rick butted in, "Jason thinks Ulysses Moore is still alive."

"Or maybe he's being held prisoner somewhere, I don't know," Jason added quickly.

Maruk remained silent for the most part. She asked questions about their lives, the strange objects that filled their world. She admitted that she'd known from the beginning that Jason and Rick were not being entirely truthful with her. "And yet," she said, "I felt that you were both good souls." She looked into Jason's eyes. "You were kind. I don't know why, but I felt that I could trust you."

They stopped at the top of the stairs that led into the storerooms of the House of Visitors. It was the moment of decision. On one side was the stairway that would take them back to where they first lost Julia. In the other direction, beyond the walls, lay the city outside . . . and the Shop of Long-Lost Maps.

Maruk watched as they hesitated. She said, "If you want to go to look for the shop, I cannot come with you," she said. "I do not have permission to go beyond the gardens of the House of Life."

"This is crazy!" Rick suddenly exclaimed, holding his head in his hands and shouting to the sky. He looked at his friends. "IT'S INSANE!"

"Well, okaaay," Jason replied. "Thanks for sharing, Rick. But the Shop of Long-Lost Maps is the only clue we've got. We don't have a choice — not really. It's as if all the decisions have already been made. The path is set. All that is left for us is to follow it to its conclusion."

"I was coming to your house for lunch," Rick complained miserably. "A ham sandwich, maybe. A little swim. That's it!"

"A sandwich?" Maruk asked.

Jason and Rick laughed. "They haven't been

invented yet," Jason said kindly. Then he joked, "Too bad, you've been missing out on Fluffernutter."

Rick made a face, holding his stomach. "You eat that garbage?"

It was enough to break the tense mood. Rick realized, despite all his doubts, that Jason was right. They had to follow the clue. After all, there was no guarantee that Julia would be back at the storeroom, or that they'd be able to find the door to the *Metis*.

Maruk finally offered a solution. "You two go ahead without me," she said. "I will go back to the storeroom. I can wait for Julia in case she comes while you're gone. Just tell me what to say."

Rick looked at Jason. It made sense.

"Yeah," Jason said after a moment. "We can do that. If Julia comes back, she'll have to pass through the same room where we met you."

Maruk smiled.

"You can tell her that . . . that Rick and I had to do something. Tell her not to worry," Jason said. "Tell her that we're fine — and that no matter what, she should stay put and wait for us."

Rick added, "Tell her that we're worried about her."

"Yeah," Jason repeated. "Tell her that we're

worried." He gently tugged on the Egyptian girl's braid. "Thank you, Maruk. You're a real friend."

After saying good-bye to Maruk, Rick and Jason headed toward the great wall that separated the House of Life from the sprawling city. They showed their scarab passes to the guards and, passing through the gate, found themselves in the vibrant city of Punt.

Immediately outside the wall, the streets were sprawling with vendors of every description. There were animals everywhere, and all for sale — bleating, mooing, screeching, and howling inside wicker cages. Some vendors sold small statues and decorative jewelry. The two boys passed by the food sellers, hawking a great variety of dishes, figs and dates, flat slabs of crunchy bread, and meat stews.

Rick strode purposefully, uncomfortable in this strange land. But Jason, more familiar with the bustle of a city, straggled behind, examining the wares, even engaging in brief conversations with the merchants.

Jason caught up with Rick, who stood open-mouthed. "Look," Rick said, "a slave market."

Before them stood a large man with ebony skin guarding four slaves who were sitting on the ground, bound together by chains. The "goods" for sale were those of flesh and blood.

"Come on," Jason prodded his friend. "Don't look — there's nothing we can do to help them."

Asking directions along the way, they finally came to a narrow alley that was packed with stands in bright, garish colors.

Jason tapped Rick's shoulder. "Look," he said. He pointed to a low brick building covered with hieroglyphics. A sign read:

SHOP OF LONG-LOST MAPS

Rick took a deep breath, working up his courage. "I guess this is the place," he said. "Let's take a look."

Jason and Rick walked down the four steps leading to the entrance. They pushed aside a curtain and entered. A strong, pungent smell of incense greeted them. The room was cluttered, disorganized. Hundreds of maps hung from thin chains attached to the ceiling. A large, low table in the center of the room was covered with papyruses depicting seas, cities, rivers, ports, and forests with exotic names.

"Wow," Rick said with awe. "This is my kind of place."

There was no sign of life. So the boys quietly made their way deeper into the store, which felt more like a dense warehouse. They brushed their fingertips over detailed charts of Babel, where every language in the world was spoken. They spotted a map of Ur, supposedly the most ancient city of mankind. On one wall was a map of a cursed town that, according to the note posted beside it, was built by men who had horns growing out of their foreheads. On the other wall, a map showed a city that was built upon the clouds, with a fragile bridge connecting it to a mountaintop. The long, twisting Nile accounted for a great number of river charts, each with information written in demotic script or with elegant, gold hieroglyphs.

"It's like a museum," Rick said.

"Yeah," Jason agreed, "a museum that preserves a world that never was, or no longer exists."

A powerful feeling of mystery touched both of them. In this place, the imaginary seemed real, the impossible seemed ordinary, and the everyday seemed magical.

They crossed into a smaller back room that was separated from the front by a heavy curtain. A booming, gravelly voice startled them. "Have you come in just to look and touch, boys, or did you come here to make me rich?"

Jason wheeled around in the direction of the voice. In the corner of the room, sitting on a lavishly

cushioned wicker armchair, was an old man with sickly, yellowed eyes and a bald head. The man's large, swollen feet were soaking in a huge bowl of hot, steaming water, alongside a lifelike statue of a crocodile that was tied to the man's chair with a sturdy rope.

"H-Hello, sir," Jason stammered, taking a step toward the old man.

But the moment he approached the shopkeeper, what he had believed to be a statue of a crocodile slowly opened its jaws in warning.

Jason froze, petrified. Behind him, Rick asked, "Is that thing alive?"

The old man cackled with delight. He rested his hand on the crocodile's snout. Upon each finger he wore large, jeweled rings. "Let's ask Talos, shall we?" the man teased. "Talos, my friend — are you alive?"

He reached into his pocket and produced what appeared to be a small piece of meat. He tossed it into the air and — *snap!* — Talos snared it with a swift, deadly bite.

"I, er, guess that answers the question," Jason said in a hushed whisper.

Talos closed his mouth again and returned to his original position. The man shifted his feet in the basin.

"So," he said, clapping his hands together, "I can see that you are travelers. Are you in need of a map, perchance?"

The boys were not sure how to answer.

The old man quickly filled the silence. "Even Talos can see that you are foreigners, and probably lost at that. But somehow you have managed to come to the right place." He laughed again, in a sudden, booming burst. He examined the boys closely, his eyes narrowing with mischief. "Strange, is it not? You were lost, but now," he opened his hands, gesturing to the maps all around him, "you are found."

Jason found the courage to speak up. "Actually, sir, we are not lost. But we are seeking . . . a map."

"That's right," Rick confirmed.

The old man burst again with laughter, his considerable belly shaking with amusement. "Then this is your lucky day. So allow me to ask — what kind of map do you seek?"

"A map of Kilmore Cove," Jason answered matter-of-factly.

"Did you hear that, Talos?" the old man inquired of his crocodile. "By the gods of Upper and Lower Egypt! What are the odds of two people coming here in search of the very same map? Within such a short time!" He clapped his hands, thoroughly

enjoying himself. "Now I am beginning to think that this must be a very important map."

"Someone has been here already?" Jason asked.

"You are correct!" The old man lifted one swollen, infected foot out of the basin, studied it with interest, then returned it to the basin. "A woman was brought here by one of my young friends," the man said. "She was a beauty, I must confess, enough to make an old man feel young again. But, I fear, a beauty that has gone quite mad." The man looked down at his reptilian house pet. "Talos did not like her, did you, Talos?"

Jason and Rick exchanged a glance. It was as they had feared. Oblivia Newton had beaten them to the shop. They needed more information.

"And what, if I may ask, did you tell her?" Jason asked politely.

"I told her exactly what I am about to tell you," said the man, shifting on his cushions. "I do not possess such a map and, as an expert in such matters, I do not even believe it exists."

Rick and Jason stared at him, uncertain of what to say next. Fortunately, the shopkeeper wasn't done yet. "If there were such a map inside the Collection, and if it was of any value, one of my boys would have found a way to — how shall I put it? — bring it to me," he explained. "Don't look so shocked, boys. In my business, it pays to have eyes and ears and light-fingered hands in many places. Many children of the streets are under my employ. I have a small army of them. They are clever, daring, and not completely honest — the three traits I value most."

"You're nothing but a thief," Jason blurted out.

Rick shot him a silencing look.

The man laughed cheerfully. "You've got a sharp tongue, boy. But not a very large brain, I'm afraid, or you would know enough to keep that tongue inside your head."

He lowered his voice to barely a whisper. "Here's some free advice, Dagger Tongue. Those who play with daggers often end up getting cut."

He lightly touched the rope leash that held the crocodile. Talos flicked his tail.

Jason scowled at the shopkeeper defiantly.

"Besides," the man continued, now in a more friendly tone, "I find the word *thief* so unpleasant. It's an ugly word. Far too crude for my liking. As I see it, it is a waste to let valuable maps rot away in the House of Life, especially when there are customers willing to pay handsomely for them." He smiled, flashing a gold tooth. "Don't you agree?"

"The House of Life is open to everyone," Rick replied.

"But the maps are not," the man said sharply. "Which is a good thing, naturally, because it keeps me in business."

"We believe that the map does exist," Jason persisted.

"That's what that angry young woman said!" the man replied. "I told her to go look for it, then. And that is what I tell you. Go ahead. Consult with those infernal Indexers. Or if you dare, try visiting the Buried Archives. Down there are things, very special items, that have not been recorded on the ledgers."

"Is that where she went?" Jason asked.

"So many questions," the man chided, "and yet such little payment." He smiled pointedly. "But, yes, I sent one of my assistants with her."

"Probably a waste of time," Jason said. He still believed the map was where Ulysses said it would be: in the Room That Isn't There.

"I agree," the man said with a shrug. A fly began to buzz around Talos's head, landing on his snout. The man watched it for a few moments before continuing. "But you see, Dagger Tongue, in one important respect she was far more appealing than you."

"Oh?"

He smiled, again flashing his gold tooth. "She was willing to pay for my services. Whereas you," he waved a hand heavy with jewelry in their direction, "offer nothing but questions. You want information — I can see that, I am not a fool — yet you give nothing in return."

"We know for a fact that the map was once stored inside the Collection," Rick interrupted. "Then it was moved to a safer place."

"Go on," the man said, suddenly interested. "I am listening."

Jason and Rick looked at each other, hesitating, as if silently trying to reach a decision. Finally, with a sigh, Jason nodded.

"We think it is hidden in the Room That Isn't There," Rick confided.

Papyrus from the
Abandoned Corridors.

The man did not smile or laugh at them. He leaned forward, bringing his hands onto the arms of his chair, as if to lift himself up. He paused there, uncertain whether rising was worth the effort it would surely require.

"Now we are getting somewhere," the man said. He fell heavily against the back of his chair. "Now that is a snake of a different color," he mused.

"What?" Jason said.

"It is beyond you, boys. You can never succeed in such a quest," the man bellowed suddenly. "Go, be gone! Get out of here! Go play astragals like the other boys. Skip stones across the water. Write love poetry to pretty girls. Do whatever you wish," he said, "but forget that you ever heard about the Room That Isn't There!"

His strong reaction stunned Rick and Jason. "You don't understand," Rick said. "It's important to us."

"Ha!" cackled the man from his chair. "Important? I'll tell you what is important — your lives! Don't endanger them chasing after something that doesn't exist!"

Rick watched as the man gave a sharp yank on the rope that held Talos. The crocodile shot forward in an instant.

Jason cried out and stepped back. But Rick did

not move. He stood still, frozen in place, waiting for the animal's charge.

Talos opened his mighty jaws, revealing rows of sharp teeth, and snapped them closed. He was mere inches away from Rick's legs.

Then, as suddenly as it had begun, the attack ended. The man gave a guttural bark and the animal backed off slowly until it was once again crouching at its master's feet.

With great effort, the old man took his feet out of the basin and pushed himself up to a standing position. He looked at Rick with admiration.

"By the gods of Upper and Lower Egypt!" he exclaimed, clapping his hands. "By the soul of my mother, may Anubis and the gods of the Afterworld protect her soul! I have never seen anything like that before. What are you, boy? A hero, a fool, or a madman?"

Rick stood still. He did not answer. Behind him, Jason watched from where he had retreated, still eyeing Talos carefully.

"I have not seen the likes of you two in all my days," the man said. Again he erupted with a short, booming laugh. He pointed at Jason, then at Rick. "Dagger Tongue and Heart of Stone! Well done, boys! I like you two!"

The shopkeeper sank back down into his chair,

settling his bruised, pus-ridden feet back into the basin of water. He gestured to two stools. "Sit," he ordered. "We will talk seriously. Man to man. Do not fear Talos, it was merely a demonstration. A little trick I taught him to scare faint-hearted boys and other pests. He would no more eat you than I would."

The boys sat down warily, still ill at ease with Talos so close.

"Dagger Tongue and Heart of Stone," the old man murmured, taking pleasure in the nicknames he had made up. "I have used that trick with Talos many times in the past," he confessed. "But never has one been so bold when facing the jaws of Talos! It seems I was mistaken about you. What do you say, lads, would you like to come work for me? I could always use new blood in my operation."

"We are not here for jobs," Jason replied. "We seek a map. That is all. Will you or will you not help us find the Room That Isn't There?"

"Ha!" the old man laughed again. "Listen to me, boys." He took a deep breath and began. "That room was once my obsession, Dagger Tongue! It was all I ever thought about, all I ever wanted. Even now, after all these years, I can still smell the fire and feel the heat of the flames." He gazed down at his injured, charred feet. "Tall, engulfing flames that sent years of work up in smoke, along with more riches than I dared dream of."

"There was a fire?" Rick asked, remembering Maruk's story. "The one that ruined part of the Collection?"

A glimmer of recognition flashed in the old man's eyes. "You have heard the story already?"

"Only a small part of it," Rick said. "Please, tell us about the fire, Mister . . . um . . ."

"You wish to know my name?" the man inquired. "Call me Mammon. Or Lucifer. Whichever you prefer."

Oblivia coughed, holding her hands over her face. "What is that horrid smell?" she complained.

"Welcome to the Buried Archives," Mammon's assistant said with a sneer. It was the same daring street urchin who had accompanied her to the Shop of Long-Lost Maps. He seemed to enjoy her discomfort.

They were inside a large underground cave, a tunnel dug into the rock and poorly illuminated by oil

lamps that let off glowing cones of dim amber light. The young man lit them one by one as they passed deeper into the cave. All around them, ruined treasures lay strewn in disarray.

"Absolutely revolting," Oblivia snapped in disgust. "How does anyone survive down here?"

"Only the lost souls survive," the boy replied mysteriously. "To stay down here for any amount of time is to become one of the walking dead."

From previous visits, Oblivia had learned how to make bribes in ancient Egypt. Gold, of course, always worked. But that was expensive. So she always left Kilmore Cove with a supply of common cigarette lighters, for they dazzled the denizens of Punt. Sometimes she traded them to a merchant in exchange for a bag full of *deben*, the local coin. And now those *deben* bought the services of every dishonest character in this strange land.

Stepping gingerly behind her guide, careful not to touch the wet walls on either side of her, Oblivia thought about the candle stub she had found in the niche. Someone had left it, obviously. And the more she thought about it, the more certain she became that it was an unknown enemy from Kilmore Cove. Ulysses Moore himself? No, he was too careful for that. And besides, the old man was dead. But who could it be? And when had they been here?

"We have arrived," the young man announced. "Our man awaits us."

Oblivia raised an eyebrow.

The young man whispered in her ear. "Hold your tongue, woman, and remark not upon his appearance. He would not meet your insults with restraint."

Oblivia caught her breath at the sight of the man, if indeed a man he was. The creature's body was lean, angular, and hideously deformed. He smelled of rancid milk, and he had pale, translucent skin that had not seen the light of day in years, if ever.

The pleasantries were brief. The man of the cave, rather than looking at her, merely sniffed. Perhaps he was blind, she guessed. Oblivia overcame her repulsion by reminding herself that this creature was a necessary evil, for it was promised that he could soon help her find the very thing she sought.

"Yesss," hissed the man of the cave, "a lady. We do not often see . . . ladiesss . . . down below. The pleasssure is oursss. What is it that you sssseek?"

The boy answered, emphasizing the name Kilmore Cove.

The translucent man nodded slowly.

The boy gestured to Oblivia that the time had come to make payment. The man's hand lashed out like a viper's tongue, snatching at the coins. He furtively deposited them into his pocket.

"Perhapsss there is sssomething for you," the creature hissed. He turned and walked with surprising agility, guiding them through the piles of objects within the Buried Archives. They made their way over broken statues and other ruins. The man crawled and climbed easily, while Oblivia stumbled and cursed under her breath. She thought she heard the scampering of small, clawed paws.

"Tell me there aren't any rats down here," Oblivia Newton muttered.

"Rats, yesss, rats aplenty," replied the man of the cave. "It is what we eat, lotsss of rats, juicy, plump, most excellent rats." He held out a hand. "Thisss way, follow closely, careful now."

The young guide stepped in line, while Oblivia struggled behind them. She thought of Manfred. She should have brought the big oaf. Manfred had limitations, but he could be useful. Oblivia fingered the candle stub inside her pocket. Just before leaving, Manfred had told her he'd seen lights from inside Salton Cliff, beneath Argo Manor.

Could it be possible? Had the door been opened again, after all these years?

I believe this sketch may reveal the secret to finding the Room That Isn't There!

Inside the Shop of Long-Lost Maps, the old man named Mammon began his tale.

"I was not always the man you see before you now," he said, "scarred and burned and, yes, plump and rich. No, I was young and eager, not unlike yourselves. I worked as an esteemed Indexer inside the Collection. I knew secrets that others never dreamed of, and all the great scholars came to me, and only to me, to locate the most ancient treasures — maps of the most distant lands, the secrets of the stars above and the dwellings below."

He idly scratched Talos on the head, his eyes closed as if searching his mind for a distant memory. "One day, a stranger appeared before me. I remember him well, though I wish I could forget him. For on that day my life took a new course. I veered from the path I had chosen. This stranger, you see, had been studying the Papyrus of the Founding of Punt, the ancient chronicles of the first men who had come here by sea and who, with the help of the gods, built the House of Life. Yes, boys, the House of Life is older than any building in Punt. Older, it is said, than the sand itself, which came years later as a curse, swept in after the Founders had vanished." He smiled, eyes open and gleaming. "But I came to wish I had never set eyes upon the Papyrus of the Founding."

"What was written there?" Jason asked.

"A mistake!" Mammon snapped. "An error, a folly, that is what was written there! The Papyrus contained a list of all the rooms in the House. But it was discovered that the list contained one extra room. A room that no Indexer had ever found. A room that not one Great Master Scribe through all the generations had known about. But I learned of it, indeed, or thought I did, when I was young and foolish.

"By reading the list, I concluded that the Papyrus had been wrong, and I informed the scholar. Yet he would not hear of it. He insisted that the room had to exist, and that the key to finding it must be hidden in some kind of riddle used to protect it. But," he laughed bitterly, "there was no riddle. Do you understand, boys? There was no riddle, just as there was no secret room. It was all an error, a mistake in the Papyrus of the Founding. It was the Room That Isn't There."

The old man moved in his chair, shifting heavily into the cushions. "For many a day, I forgot all about the scholar. I tried to put aside thoughts of a secret room, a room that no one knew. Then, the man returned. He confided to me, his esteemed Indexer, that he had solved the riddle that had kept the room from all prying eyes."

"What was the riddle?" Rick asked.

Mammon leaned in close and wet his lips. "Only this: *It is on everyone's lips and under everyone's nose!* What a fool — that is what the scholar told me. And do you know why he said that? To challenge me! To corrupt me! To drive me nearly insane! After all, I was the finest of the Indexers."

Mammon opened his arms expansively. "And so I began my search — an empty journey that has turned me into this: a bitter, broken old man whose only pleasure is the company of a cold-blooded crocodile."

"I don't get it," Jason said. "Why did you believe the scholar? There must have been a good reason."

"The heart believes what it wants to believe," Mammon said. "The scholar told me, 'When you find the room, you'll see the symbol of the three turtles.'"

"Three turtles?" Jason murmured. He remembered the symbol on the archway over the door in the grotto. Three turtles.

Mammon gazed at Jason's face sagely, as if reading the boy's mind. "Do you know of it, Dagger Tongue? Have you seen it before?"

"Yes," Jason confessed. "I have seen three turtles once, in my travels."

"Then you are more fortunate than I am, or more unfortunate," Mammon answered. "I myself never found it. And I looked, oh, I searched for months and years. I began to neglect my duties. My colleagues came to despise me. Such vanity! Such greed! I searched for that room only to prove — what? That I was better than anyone else? That I was equal to the Founders? That I was a great explorer, the greatest of them all?" The old man sighed, a weary look on his face. "I cannot answer, for what man can truly tell the secrets of his own dark heart?"

"It was a riddle," Jason said kindly. "You wanted to solve it — maybe you needed to solve it. That doesn't make you a bad person."

The old man nodded, the faintest of smiles on his lips. "You are kind," he said. "Too kind. For I was consumed by anger over my failures. I searched the corridors of the House day and night. I mapped out every passageway and secret staircase, until I knew every corner and every door. I am ashamed to say that I could think of no one else, not even of one whom I once loved.

"Don't you see?" he said. "The riddle destroyed me. Broke my heart. Ruined my life!"

He poured himself a glass of water and drank deeply. His eyes were filled with a great sadness.

Jason and Rick glanced at each other, wondering if that was the end of the story.

But Mammon continued. "Spurred by that riddle, that dream of a room that did not exist, I came to know the House of Life as if it were my own soul. And what good has it done me? My feet are ruined, my legs cry out in pain with each step. Whatever secrets I know are of little use to me. It's a cruel joke that Fate played upon me, the fool. Yes, I can send my boys anytime, anywhere. I have taught them every corridor, every passageway. But I promise you, there is no such thing as the Room That Isn't There!"

"The fire," Jason reminded him. "What about the fire?"

The shopkeeper hung his head in sorrow. "The final time I went into the Collection as an Indexer, I was convinced I had solved the riddle. *It was on everyone's lips*, the scholar had said. I thought I knew the answer. So I ran off into the House, ignoring my duties. I thought I knew what to do!" he admitted. "I was certain of the answer! Oh wretched vanity, I dared match wits with the gods!"

His voice grew ominous, his words softer. Jason and Rick leaned in to hear. "That night I slept inside the House and waited for dawn. And I moved the mirrors. That was the key! The mirrors redirected the sunbeams — and the rays, the rays set the papy- ruses on fire. That, my young friends, was how the fire broke out. It was all my fault! For the moment the first papyrus caught fire, a sudden wind fed the flames, driving them from niche to niche, from scroll to scroll, from table to table. In moments, that whole wing of the Collection was engulfed in flames!"

The shop room had grown dark around them. The old man finished his story. "I was injured, ruined, driven out of the House forever. I took ref- uge here and set up my little shop of broken dreams. I take money from fools, for it is easily gotten."

A long, reflective silence followed. Each sat alone, lost in his own private thoughts.

"What was the solution?" Rick finally asked.

The old man grumbled. "Heart of Stone listens, but he does not hear. Have you learned nothing? Have I wasted my breath all this time? There is no riddle," he spat scornfully. "No secret room. And no map!"

"But you said . . ."

"I said," Mammon howled, rising, "THE ROOM DOESN'T EXIST!" At his feet, Talos stirred, unsettled.

Jason got up from his stool. "Thank you, sir, for

telling us this sad story. You have given us much to think about. We will go now to read this Papyrus of the Founding."

The man let out a scornful laugh. "How? It can't be done. The Papyrus of the Founding is lost forever. It was burned to ashes in the fire, along with every other reference to the Room That Isn't There."

"We won't give up," Rick said with determination.

"Then you are fools like me, bent on destroying your lives," Mammon replied. He scratched Talos's head slowly, deep in thought. "But I am a businessman," he said at last. "Perhaps, for one final clue, we can make an arrangement."

Manfred prowled the gardens of Argo Manor, howling and cursing in anger. He pounded on the kitchen door, banged on the front door, beat against the windows of the portico. Everything was shut tight. Yet his fury persisted.

Julia covered her ears. "What does he want?" she asked Nestor. "Does it have to do with the door?"

A different type of fury burned inside Nestor. Not the wild raging of a youthful brute, but the cold resolution of an old man. Manfred was an attacker, a hunter. But Nestor's strength was that of a defender. He stood with Julia, determined to protect her.

Julia was the first to notice the change. The screaming had stopped. Outside: only wind and rain. Where was Manfred? She whispered to Nestor, "Maybe he went away."

A quick glance out the front windows showed that the dark car was still in the courtyard.

Nestor did not say a word. He kept close to Julia, trailing behind her like a shadow, his face hardened with anger. For the first time since she had come to Argo Manor, Julia realized that Nestor was an old man. Fragile, vulnerable. He could not save her.

"What do you think he's doing?" she asked.

Nestor held her hand. He walked up the stairs and opened the mirrored door to the tower. Julia paused by the door. Nestor went inside. He peered down at the garden from every window.

Julia noticed that someone had used a wooden wedge to reinforce the broken latch on the tower window. "Who is he, Nestor?" she asked again with a frightened voice. "Why is he doing this to us?"

"It is an old story," Nestor said with a sigh.

"Tell it to me."

"Not now, child."

"Yes, now," Julia demanded. "Tell it to me — right now."

The wind howled outside.

"It was a terrible mistake," Nestor said. "A mistake that Penelope — Mrs. Moore — made a long time ago. You see, she had hoped to make Kilmore Cove a little more modern."

"Modern?" Julia echoed. "When Jason and I first got here, we thought time had stopped."

The caretaker of Argo Manor chuckled softly. "No," he said with a weary shake of his head. "Time comes and wounds us all. Even at Argo Manor."

Nestor checked the other windows on the second floor, hoping to catch a glimpse of the intruder below. He and Julia moved to the master bedroom, where her parents slept. Nestor opened the shutters. He was looking out through the rain, waiting for the beacon from the lighthouse to pass by so he could see more clearly.

Julia stared at the darkened room, all in shadow. "What mistake did Mrs. Moore make?" she asked.

Nestor closed the shutters. "Mrs. Moore invited some people over for tea," he said. "Mr. Moore did not think it was a good idea, but Mrs. Moore . . . ah, she was a trusting person, unable to think ill of anyone. That," he said, looking Julia in the eye, "was her mistake. She underestimated the cruelty that exists in the world."

"The man outside," Julia said. "Was he invited into the house?"

"He's only a henchman, a stooge," Nestor said with scorn. "At least, that is what I thought until tonight."

"So he has been here before?" Julia asked. The wind howled, heavy with rain.

"Yes, yes," Nestor nodded. "But never inside! He drove his boss, Oblivia Newton. She was the one who came inside. Only once — but it was one time too many. After that day, she was never allowed to return."

Julia understood. "She wants the house," she said.

Nestor's eyes narrowed. He nodded once.

A loud crash came from outside.

"The toolshed!" Nestor exclaimed. "He is trying to get into the toolshed!"

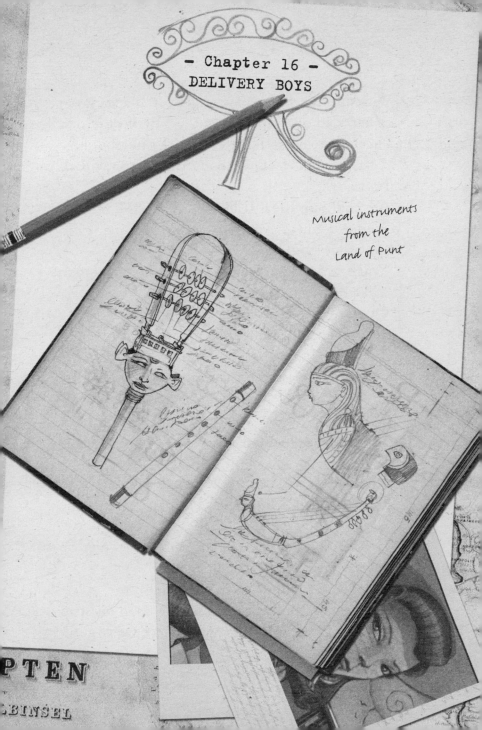

Musical instruments
from the
Land of Punt

Outside the Shop of Long-Lost Maps, Jason puzzled over the map of the city of Punt that had been sketched in Ulysses Moore's notebook.

"I have a bad feeling about this, Jason," Rick murmured.

"Oh chill out, Rick. It'll be okay," Jason replied. "Why don't you give me a hand with this map? I'm lousy with these things."

"You heard the old man's story," Rick protested. "It's like he was trying to warn us."

"Or scare us away," Jason said defiantly.

Rick sighed and studied the map, then looked up to check his bearings. Men and women wearing bright clothing passed by without a second glance. But even so, Rick felt exposed in the city, uncomfortable around so many people. He couldn't shake the feeling that something bad was about to happen.

"Look," Jason said calmly. "It's just two deliveries, that's all. It will be fun. What can happen?"

Rick shrugged. "I just have a bad feeling," he repeated. "I can't explain it."

"He said that he'd give us the final clue when we returned," Jason said. "The final clue!"

"What if he's lying?" Rick retorted.

"It's a chance I'm willing to take," Jason insisted. "After all, right now it's the only chance we've got."

Rick eyed an obelisk in the middle of the square. It marked the intersection of four dirt roads. He squinted down at the map. A smile slowly formed on his lips as he realized which way they needed to go. He looked at Jason, then pointed at the obelisk. "Well, what are waiting for? The port is thataway!"

Mammon had given the boys two leather parcels that, he claimed, contained maps. The first was to be delivered to the captain of a Phoenician ship. The second was for a *semu*, or doctor, who was organizing an expedition in search of rare herbs and spices for his remedies.

The port wasn't difficult to find. To the east of the obelisk, the city of Punt sloped down to a series of piers and wharves that formed the harbor. The Phoenician ship had a tapered underbelly and a bow that reminded the boys of the *Metis*. The captain, a man from Syria, had long, black hair and a muscular body. He greeted the boys in a friendly manner.

"So, you must be Mammon's two new helpers!" he said.

Rick handed him the roll of papyrus and nodded. "She is a beautiful ship, sir," he said, admiring the masts and oar fittings with the eye of an expert.

"Where are you headed?" Jason asked.

"The port of Mycenae, sailing along the coast as

far as we can." The captain unrolled the papyrus at their feet. "Fine, fine, excellent work."

He tipped the boys with a handful of *deben* and sent them on their way. Moments later, Rick and Jason bought rolls of unleavened bread, filled with a hot mixture of mutton, spices, vegetables, and fish. They sat with their feet dangling off the pier and gobbled down their late-afternoon meal.

But there was little time for delay. The boys hurried to make their second delivery. And Rick learned that it was easy to navigate his way around Punt. The colossal walls of the House of Life could be seen from practically every intersection. The roads formed a basic grid, with the larger avenues serving to help distinguish the various neighborhoods.

While searching for the person to whom they had to deliver the package, the boys happened upon a small crowd of people gathered around two musicians who were performing "The Ballad of Two Lovers." One of the musicians, his face painted white, plucked a stringed instrument and, from time to time, would blow into a wooden flute. The other, dressed in black, his face smeared with dark clay, was passionately shaking tambourines and rattling another instrument the boys had never seen before.

Jason and Rick listened to a few verses of the song before they realized that this was the same legend about the two lovers who had been lost in the House of Life. "We should hurry up. Let's go," Rick finally said to Jason. The boys moved on. They recognized the *semu*'s house by the long line of people waiting in the outer courtyard. Men, women, children, and elderly people were all patiently waiting their turns for a visit with the doctor.

"I guess some things never change," Jason joked. "A typical doctor's waiting room — except this guy makes the patients wait outside. The only thing missing is *Highlights* magazine."

"Goofus and Gallant!" Rick said with a laugh, remembering two popular comic-strip characters from the magazine. "I used to love finding the objects that were hidden in the picture."

"See?" Jason noted. "You loved mysteries even then!"

The boys passed through the crowd, explaining that they were messengers. Inside the house, they were greeted by a room filled with exotic aromas. Two boys with shaved heads watched over tubs of hot water. There was a row of assorted plants and, beyond them, endless vials filled high with powders of every color.

The doctor was preparing a poultice for a woman who had scraped her shin. When he saw the boys come in, he recognized the papyrus Jason held in his hand. Ignoring the woman, he barked out, "The map! What took you so long? Give it here!"

He rudely snatched the map out of Jason's hand and, without so much as a nod, turned his back to the boys.

Jason cleared his throat. It was something he'd seen done when he had traveled with his parents. Maybe the doctor would give them a tip. He was still a little hungry.

"Are you waiting for a tip?" the doctor sputtered angrily. "You were late! Get out — now. And be thankful I don't have you whipped!"

Jason and Rick quickly scrambled off. "What a jerk," Rick muttered.

"Yeah, he's not exactly a people person, is he?" Jason replied. "But who cares? Let's get back to the shop and find out about that clue."

"You *must* be joking," Oblivia Newton said, her voice dripping with disgust. "There's no way I'm getting into that thing."

The underground man had led them to a vertical shaft that dropped far below until it was swallowed whole by darkness. To the sides were dozens of tunnels connected to one another by pulleys, boards, and odd transports made of wood and rope.

"It looks as if it was built by a madman," Oblivia remarked.

The underground man gave a low, mirthless snicker. Once again, he cocked his head to the makeshift trolley before them. It was simply a small platform without walls, tied to four very thick — but very old — ropes.

"Yesss, use it we mussst," the mole-man said. He invited Oblivia to climb onto the platform. The ropes extended all the way across the pit. At the other end was a tunnel that promised to be even darker than the one from which they had come. "What you ssseek is on the other sssside," the underground man explained. "Come, go, stay, leave. It isss not for me to decide. If you ssseek transssport, you must pay for transssport."

Oblivia glared at her young Egyptian guide, who smiled at her dispassionately. "You go ahead," he said. "I'll wait here."

"Every ounce the gentleman," Oblivia sneered. She produced more *deben* from her pocket. The

underground man snatched them from her with slippery swiftness — the way a gecko catches a gnat.

"Yesss, now into the transsssport," he lisped.

Oblivia rested the tip of her foot on top of the wooden board, which creaked and pitched dangerously to the side. With a startled cry, she clung to the rope, just barely saving herself from a nasty fall into the abyss below.

"Careful, tsssk, tsssk," the underground man said. "Hold on to the ropesss. Very nice, pretty lady."

Oblivia grabbed a rope with each hand.

"And now, we go," the underground man said, pushing the platform. Then he deftly hopped onto the wooden board beside her and released the jam, which careened downward. The platform groaned and tilted, jerking awkwardly along the main rope. Oblivia felt her stomach turn. She was too scared to scream.

In the span of mere moments, they were on the other side of the pit, staring into a tunnel that was almost pitch-black. Little by little, Oblivia's eyes grew accustomed to the darkness. The tunnel was full of clay jars.

The underground man sniffed the air, scrunching his nose like a ferret. Moving swiftly, he made his way between two rows of large pots. "Come," he ordered. "But watch your ssstep."

Oblivia hesitated before following. Her young guide waved to her mockingly from the other side of the pit. Determined not to give him the satisfaction of seeing her terrified, she turned back toward the tunnel and set out to follow the underground man. She soon stepped on something squishy and wriggly. It squeaked and scampered out from beneath her footfall.

"Don't be afraid, pretty lady," the underground man's voice echoed from the darkness ahead. "Rats very sssmall, and they scurry away if you walk ssslowly. But ssspiders don't run much. Spiders just squish." He laughed. "Poor creatures, sssealed down here in the dark underground. Pitiful monsters. But are not dangerousss."

"I demand that you get me out of this horrible hole immediately!" Oblivia commanded.

The underground man lifted the lid off one of the jars. "Here," he announced. "Here is sssomething!"

For Oblivia, the next few moments were a blur. She felt faint, unable to breathe. A great dizziness came over her. Without remembering how, she once again found herself back on the platform, shuttling across the abyss, with the underground man's grotesque hand on her back, steadying her.

The young Egyptian was standing before her.

"How did you enjoy that, Ms. Newton?" he asked solicitously. "Care for another ride?"

Oblivia glared at him, her mind still reeling. "Take me out of here, I beg you," she pleaded. "I feel ill."

"Misunderstood creaturesss," the underground man whispered. "Ratsss and sssnakes mean no harm."

Oblivia shook her head violently, as if trying to cast this place out of her memory.

"Yesss," the underground man hissed. "Thisss place is my home. It disssgusts you, pretty lady? You do not wish to ssstay for a longer visit?"

He handed Oblivia a large, dark parcel on which a series of hieroglyphs were scrawled in red ink.

Oblivia read the carefully lettered words: *Place of origin: Kilmore Cove.*

Her eyes cleared, her heart leaped. She looked at the underground man. "I knew there was sssomething in the Buried Archives," he said.

Oblivia anxiously opened the parcel. It contained a small thin object made of paper. A business card.

The Egyptian stood by her side. "Is that it?"

"No!" Oblivia Newton thundered. "This is not at all what I sought! I came all the way down here to find . . . this? This crummy, stupid little card?! I didn't need to travel to Egypt to find the address of a hair stylist from Kilmore Cove!"

GWENDALINE MAINOFF

St. Patrick Large n° 18 - 74820 Kilmore Cove

The underground man licked his lips, smirking. "Yesss, but if the pretty lady wantsss," he offered. "You may ssstay for snacksss."

Oblivia's face filled with disgust. "This is it? This is all there is in the archives? A hairdresser's business card?!" Oblivia clenched her fists with rage. "Ulysses Moore!" she seethed. "You taunt me even from the grave!"

Oblivia wheeled toward her guide. "Take me out of this place, away from this . . . disgusting creature!" she shouted. "Bring me back to the Shop of Long-Lost Maps. I want to talk to your boss! Now!"

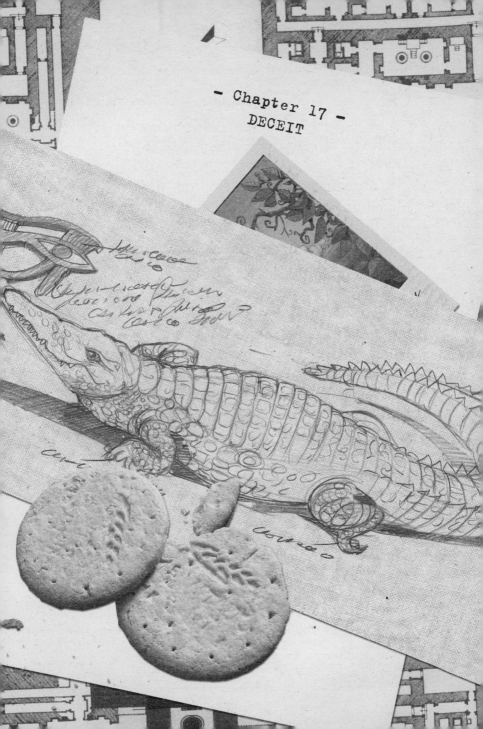

The shopkeeper, Mammon, was dozing in the same wicker chair, waiting patiently for Jason and Rick's arrival. At his side, strangely restless, was Talos.

Rick coughed upon entering the shop, and Mammon instantly awakened. Jason explained that they had made the deliveries. "Now it is time for you to live up to your end of the bargain," he said boldly.

"Ha!" Mammon laughed. "Dagger Tongue has spoken. And Dagger Tongue is right! I must keep my promise." He scratched his chin and winked at them. "I forget — what is it you wished to know again?"

"The clue," Rick said, "to the Room That Isn't There!" Rick scanned the dark corners of the room. Something wasn't right. He sniffed the air . . . incense and another sweet smell, a strangely familiar scent. . . .

The old man cleared his throat. He spat noisily into the basin where he soaked his feet. "But it isn't there, so what can my clue be worth to you?"

Jason was stone-faced. "You promised," he said.

"And what if I lied?" the old man shot back. "Did that never occur to you? You never thought that a horrible old man with rotting flesh might have tricked you?! Are you so young that you can be fooled that easily? You know, after all, it is how I make my living."

"Yes, separating fools from their money," Rick replied, glancing unhappily at Jason. "It crossed our minds."

"I think you are going to give us the clue," Jason said.

The old man's eyes widened in mock surprise. "Oh? And why would I do that?" he asked. "You already delivered my maps for free. I have no need to repay you with a favor."

"You are a businessman," Jason answered, "and you must honor the deal. Besides, I believe that you are still curious about the Room That Isn't There."

"Nonsense!"

"Somewhere deep inside of you," Jason said, "that curious Indexer is still there. You still dream of it, because old dreams never die."

Mammon nodded, momentarily speechless. "Perhaps," he mused. "Or perhaps not. I assure you that my dream died long ago." He clapped his hands together. "Still, you are right about one thing. I am a businessman. A bargain is a bargain. I will tell you my little secret."

He leaned forward. "Do you know of a song called 'The Ballad of Two Lovers?'"

Jason and Rick nodded.

"Of course you do," the old man continued. "Everyone in Punt knows it. That song is on everyone's lips. Well, it might be that the solution to the riddle can be found in the last stanza of that ballad!"

After a hurried good-bye, the boys threw back the curtain to the doorway and disappeared into the bazaar.

As they strode away, Rick kept thinking about the old man's last words: "Be careful who you trust, boys. After all, I am he who set fire to the Collection!"

At that moment, two figures stepped out from behind a shadowy curtain inside the shop.

"Ugh," Oblivia Newton complained. "What a foul stench! I couldn't have survived back there another moment!"

The old man laughed. "Did you hear that, Talos?" he said, stroking the crocodile between the eyes. "The lady here doesn't like the smell of your bedroom."

Oblivia Newton walked to the front of the shop, raised the curtain cautiously, and took a deep breath. Then she turned back to the old man named Mammon.

Talos twitched, watching her with cold eyes.

"I would not step any closer," Mammon advised his guest, holding the crocodile's leash lightly in his fingers. "Did you recognize the boys?"

Oblivia nodded.

"And?"

"It was them," Oblivia answered. "But there should have been three of them. One of them is missing — a girl. The thin boy's twin sister."

"Dagger Tongue has a twin?" Mammon cackled. "Imagine two of them!"

Oblivia sneered. "His name is Jason Covenant. The other boy is just a simpleton from town — Rick Banner, a fisherman's son."

"Watch your tongue!" the old man warned. "I am a fisherman's son."

"They were the ones who stole the map from under my nose!" Oblivia complained.

"I would not be so sure of that," said the young man who had guided her this far. "It sounds like they are still looking for it themselves."

"Did I ask your opinion?" Oblivia shot back in vexation.

The old man laughed, clearly enjoying the show. "An angry woman and a young man snapping at each other like street curs," he said. "What a wonderful day this is!" He clapped his hands. "What

you two need is a plan. And what I need, of course, is a little motivation. Money, in other words." He held up a finger, silencing Oblivia's protest. "Dagger Tongue and Heart of Stone are convinced that the map is hidden in the Room That Isn't There. They have just set off to look for it."

Oblivia frowned. "You mean to tell me all that gibberish you told them was true?"

The old man twisted in his cushioned throne. "By all the gods of Upper and Lower Egypt, how can I make you people understand? There is no clue. Don't you see? Don't you understand? The Room That Isn't There . . . well, IT ISN'T THERE!"

Lyrics to "The Ballad of Two Lovers"

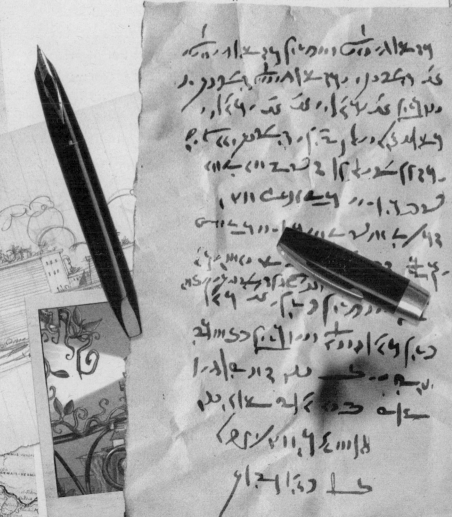

The boys reunited with Maruk, who had been waiting in the storage room. No one had moved the board that covered up the hole. Julia had not returned.

The three adventurers emerged outside and sat by a fountain. From that vantage point, they could see the House of Visitors and, in case Maruk's father appeared, the entrance to the House of Life.

Maruk shook her head in disbelief. "He got you to work for free," she said of the shop owner, "in exchange for an empty promise."

Jason was far more hopeful. "But you told us that no one has ever explored the entire Collection," he pointed out. "There are thousands of corridors. Why can't there also be a Room That Isn't There?"

Rick quickly jotted a series of calculations on a piece of paper. "To be exact," he noted, "inside the walls alone there should be ten thousand, six hundred, and forty-eight corridors. That's twenty-two sections times twenty-two rooms times twenty-two corridors. . . ."

He bent his head over the page, quickly figuring the math.

"Don't forget the secret passages," Jason said. "Mammon said that he knew of hundreds of secret passages! Those walls must have been built in different phases, and every architect might have created his own little secret. A niche here or there, an extra stairway . . ."

"Yes," Maruk admitted. "That is possible."

Rick looked up, beaming. He announced, "Five hundred and fifty-three thousand, six hundred and ninety-six niches! If we spent one minute exploring each niche . . ."

Jason rolled his eyes, grinning at Maruk.

Maruk twirled her braid around her finger. "Still, I do not believe in this room of yours. The old man who told you all that is a thief. You were foolish to trust him. If you dare mention the name Mammon to an official at the Collection, he'll make the sign of Horus to ward off bad luck."

"Yes, but there was something about him that was tragic," Jason replied. "His life had a lot of sadness to it."

Maruk answered, "Yes, his soul has been corrupted from years of dishonesty and lies. He is the Indexer who set an entire section of documents on fire!"

"He admitted it," Jason said. For some reason he felt the need to defend Mammon. "I don't know, Maruk. I like the guy."

Maruk frowned unhappily. "You should be more careful about the friends you make," she warned. "That man is dangerous, believe me. How he has

managed to avoid a death sentence is beyond me. Everyone knows he is a thief, yet he has never been caught in the act."

"Okay," Jason replied. "We have a difference of opinion. So let's talk about something else. What can you tell us about the ballad? Do you know all the words?"

"It is only a song," Maruk replied. "Everyone sings it differently. The words have changed over the years. Each singer adds something new, takes something away. Besides," she added with a note of frustration, "how can it possibly contain an important clue? It's a song that everyone knows!"

"That's exactly the point!" Jason said eagerly. "Sometimes the best place to hide something is out in the open, right under everyone's nose!"

Rick suddenly emerged from his frantic scribbling. "Okay. According to my calculations it would take us seven hundred and sixty-eight days to explore just the main section within the walls! That's not counting secret passageways or unknown niches."

Jason and Maruk looked at him, astonished. Then they laughed out loud.

Rick watched them, puzzled. Then he grinned. "So, um, what were you two just talking about?"

At Jason's urging, Maruk again explained "The Ballad of Two Lovers."

"It is about two people who search the House for the meaning of life. But the moment they set out, the man turns down one corridor, and the woman goes in a different direction," she told the boys. "They become lost. From that moment on, the two wander around without ever finding each other again."

"I guess the song is saying that it's impossible to find the meaning of life," Jason concluded.

"Or that it is impossible to find it by looking all on your own," Rick countered. "Maybe the meaning of life is found in our relationships with one another."

Maruk nodded. "Love," she said. "The two lovers should never have parted."

"How does the song end?" Jason asked.

Maruk shut her eyes for a moment, softly humming the melody in an effort to recall the words. She said, "The man and the woman are convinced that, sooner or later, they will find a place where they will meet again. Their search will end in the Room That Isn't There."

Jason looked at Rick. "There you go!"

"But I thought the ballad finishes without the two lovers ever finding the room," Rick said.

"Oh stop it," Jason complained. "You can be so negative sometimes. Anyway, I think that room really does exist. And inside it ... Ulysses hid the map!"

Maruk went off in search of an accurate transcription of the words to the ballad. She quickly returned, kneeling on the ground as she unrolled the long text. "According to my music teacher," Maruk told the boys, "this is the oldest and most precise version of the ballad."

Three pairs of eyes quickly scanned down to the last stanza:

Reached through a curtain made of light sublime,
our room is unlocked with a vibrant key.
There we shall meet at the coinciding time
of lover chasing lover for eternity.

Jason sat up, running his hands through his hair. "Okay, Rick. This one is up to you."

Rick stared at Jason, mouth agape. "Why is it my job?"

Jason tapped a finger on his forehead. "You're the one with brains," he said. "I'm the guy to go to for wild intuition, daredevil risks, and strokes of good luck. Intelligence, good old-fashioned brain power — that's your department!"

Jason turned to Maruk and confided, "This will only take him a minute. You'll see."

"Jason, cut it out!" Rick snapped. "At least try to give me a hand, would you?"

"Does this stanza mean anything to you?" Jason asked Maruk. "Is there any reference to something you've heard about in the House of Life? Or, I don't know, some other freaky legend of Punt? Think hard, Maruk."

Maruk leaned over the papyrus, carefully reading and rereading the final stanza. But in the end, she shook her head. "I'm sorry, Jason. Nothing comes to mind."

"And yet," Jason said, "according to Mammon, this stanza explains how to get into that room."

"Okay, I'll play along," Rick said. "Let's say that this room exists. It has to be *somewhere*, right? So the song has to tell us how to get there." He paused. "Maybe."

"Go on," Jason said.

"Maybe it also says *when* you can get there," Maruk pointed out. "Look, right here it says . . . *the coinciding time*."

"To coincide," Jason murmured. "Maybe it's two things that happen at the same time? Or things that fit together perfectly?" He turned to Rick. "What kinds of things coincide?"

"Train schedules," Rick said. "Puzzle pieces . . . fingers in clasped hands . . . jaws of teeth . . ."

"What else coincides?" Jason asked, racking his brain.

Rick thought for a moment. "We need at least two things," he said slowly. "Two things that come together, perfectly synchronized. The way clock hands meet at the hour of midnight!"

"Right," Jason said, "that's a good one. And we've got two lovers. They will meet at the coinciding time. The hour when two things come together."

"You're getting there," cheered Maruk. "Maybe this makes sense after all!"

The three kids continued to read and reread the stanza. Rick even scanned the entire ballad, but it didn't help. They were stumped.

"The room doesn't have a door," Jason said after a while. "It says that it has *a curtain made of light*. If there's a curtain, then there probably isn't a door — like in the Shop of Long-Lost Maps. When you've crossed through the curtain . . . you're already inside."

Rick nodded. "That's good thinking, Jason. Okay, no door. And if Maruk is right, we have to find the room at the right time."

"Could the curtain be a beam of sunlight?" Maruk

asked, suddenly inspired. "Maybe the room is in darkness, and the light only reaches the entrance?"

"Or just the opposite," Rick said. "The song says *light sublime.* Sublime can mean beautiful, or complete, or absolute."

"It also means majestic," Maruk said. "Like in a temple. Something holy."

"Yes," Rick agreed. "Something sublime can be lofty or elevated, like light coming down through the ceiling, maybe."

They sat in silence, straining to find the answer to what seemed like an impossible riddle.

"Let's move on," Rick said. "We're getting hung up on this part. If it doesn't have a door . . . then why would you need a key?"

"A vibrant key," Maruk noted.

"A key that is bright and colorful?" Jason asked.

"Or one that . . . vibrates?" Rick said.

"What about the keys on a piano?" Jason guessed.

Rick raised his eyebrows hopefully, then sighed. "Unfortunately, the piano won't be invented for several centuries," he said. "No, the vibrant key must be some kind of real key. A key that opens a door? Or a window?"

Jason groaned. "I think my head is going to

explode!" He threw himself on the grass in frustration.

Maruk stood up and stretched. "Let's take a break. I think we need it. Besides, it is almost sunset. I'm starting to get cold." She shivered.

"What did you say?" Jason asked, lifting his head from the grass.

"She's starting to get cold," Rick answered for Maruk. "In the desert there's a huge temperature change between night and day."

"That's it!" Jason exclaimed. He jumped to his feet. "That's the coinciding time! Why didn't we think of it before?"

Rick and Maruk exchanged a baffled look.

"It's so obvious!" Jason continued. "We kept thinking of the two lovers in the song as a man and a woman. But forget that. Don't think of them as two lovers in flesh and blood, but as something different. Like the sun and the moon, for example. Or the sun and the earth!"

Rick was stunned by the idea. "The two eternal lovers who can never meet," he said. Then he repeated a line from the final stanza: "*Lover chasing lover for eternity!*"

"They couldn't be the sun and the moon," Maruk objected, "because those would be the gods Amen-Re and Thoth. It can't be the sun and the earth, either, because the earth is the god Geb."

"Think about two different things that come together . . . at a coinciding time," Rick emphasized. "Let's stay focused."

"Sunrise!" cried Maruk.

"Or sunset!" Rick added excitedly. "But the stanza doesn't tell us which one it is."

It was Jason's turn to contribute. "But remember the story that Mammon told us? He said that he slept overnight in the House . . . and that he moved the mirrors!"

"Yes!" Rick exclaimed. "It had to be dawn. Maruk is right. Sunrise!"

"No," Jason said. "That's where he made his final mistake. Mammon believed that he would find the curtain of light at dawn — but he was wrong! The morning sunlight, reflected off the mirrors he mentioned, caused the great fire. The coinciding time isn't sunrise, it's sunset!"

Rick glanced at the falling sun. "That's really soon," he said.

"And we still have no idea where to go," Maruk pointed out.

"We have to look where Mammon looked," Jason replied. "The Abandoned Corridors!"

Nestor peered out the window. "What is he doing?" he asked Julia, trusting her younger eyes.

The two were huddled in a small bathroom on the second floor, which had the only window that could give them a clear view of the toolshed.

"He hasn't managed to get in," Julia replied. "Wait! I think he's giving up. He's looking back at the house, waving his arms like a crazy person."

Indeed, Manfred shook his fists toward the bolted windows of Argo Manor. He raged above the storm. "I'll get inside soon enough," he roared. "You just wait and see!" Then he disappeared from view.

Julia and Nestor hurried from room to room, racing to other windows, desperately trying to figure out where Manfred had gone.

"I don't see him anywhere," Julia said in a low voice.

They heard two loud blows against the kitchen door.

"Well," Nestor managed to joke, "at least we can hear him." He looked at Julia for a long moment. "You are a brave girl. Do you know that?"

"Yep," Julia replied, "but I wish I didn't have to be."

Manfred rattled all of the doorknobs on the ground floor once again. Finally, he retreated to the shelter of his car. Julia heard the car door open. She saw the light turn on inside.

"Maybe he's giving up," she said hopefully. "Maybe he'll go away."

Manfred switched on the car radio. He turned on rock music at full volume.

"Cool, Green Day," Julia murmured in appreciation.

The light inside the car turned off.

"He crawled out on the other side," Nestor muttered. "The dumb brute thinks he can trick us. He wants us to believe that he's still in the car."

On the far side of the garden, beyond the car, was the guesthouse where Nestor lived, the caretaker's quarters. Suddenly, Nestor dashed away from the window.

"Nestor, where are you going?!" Julia shouted.

He didn't answer.

Julia followed him as he went down the stairs, through the sitting room, and into the kitchen. He paused at the back door.

"Don't go out there!" Julia pleaded. "You might get hurt."

"Julia, listen to me," he said solemnly. "Whatever happens, whatever you see through the window, do

not leave the safety of this house. He can't get in here. Do you understand?"

Julia nodded.

"I cannot allow him to break into my quarters," Nestor said. "He cannot, he must not. Julia, I know I can count on you. Rick and Jason need you to stay here inside the house."

"Don't leave," Julia repeated. She reached for his arm.

Nestor scanned the kitchen quickly. "Don't be afraid," he told Julia. "You are not alone."

He opened the kitchen door. A gust of wind ripped it from his hand, blowing the door wide open. Nestor tucked his head down and walked into the storm.

Julia pulled the door shut and locked it. Then she raced back upstairs where she could watch from a second-floor window.

"Mom, Dad, Jason, Rick," she said under her breath in a sort of prayer. "Mom, Dad, Jason, Rick," she repeated, finding comfort in the words.

She stopped at the doorway to the sitting room. The beacon from the lighthouse swept over the garden. Someone was out there, moving quickly through the shadows.

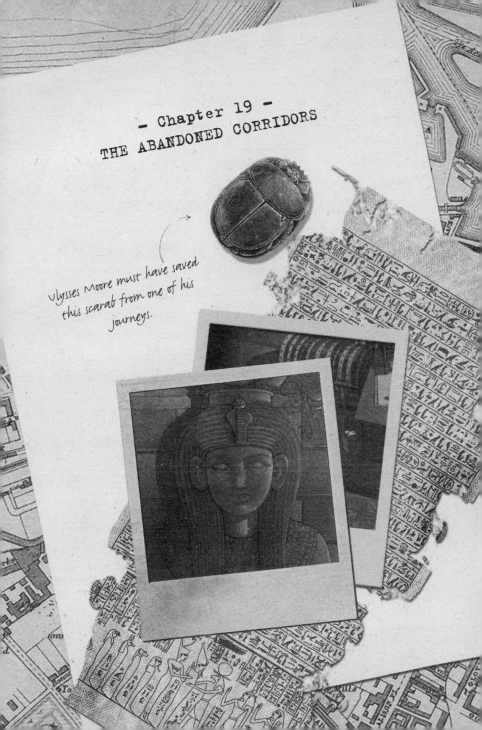

- Chapter 19 -
THE ABANDONED CORRIDORS

Ulysses Moore must have saved this scarab from one of his journeys.

The heavy door to the Abandoned Corridors opened with a creak, revealing a vast, empty room.

"As far as I know, no one has set foot in here for years," Maruk said, pausing at the threshold. "Basically, since the fire . . ."

An eerie silence engulfed them. Jason and Rick took a few, halting steps forward. They could feel a forbidding presence all around them — of pain, ashes, and despair, of things dead and lost and long forgotten. The walls and ceiling were covered with soot marks that looked like scars made by massive claws. The statues of the gods that once decorated the room had been reduced to twisted shadows, blackened by soot; their animal faces, once fierce and noble, now looked ruined and desecrated.

Not even the immense window looking out over the inner courtyard seemed to offer any solace to the place. It was as if the fetid air had remained perfectly still, poisoned, unable to circulate.

To Jason, Maruk, and Rick, it felt like they were entering a tomb.

Jason lit an oil lamp. Beside him, Rick opened the *Dictionary of Forgotten Languages*. Jason held up the lamp and saw row upon row of burned-out niches. He gasped audibly. The destruction was overwhelming. The room itself felt like the cradle of death.

"It's like being in an underground cemetery," Jason whispered. He forced himself not to think of the countless comic books he had read, stories in which a skeleton's bony hands lunged out from the shadows.

Maruk still hesitated on the threshold, unsure whether or not to enter. She had been raised to think of the Abandoned Corridors as forbidden, a place where there was nothing to see except ashes and destruction.

"Are you coming?" Jason asked, when he realized she was lagging behind out of nervousness. He held out a hand.

"I don't know if I can go through with this," she said. "Today I've broken practically every rule that my father established in the House of Life."

"So one more won't kill you," Jason said encouragingly. He clasped her fingers in his hand. "Come on."

Maruk shut her eyes. When she opened them, Jason was at her side. His face was lit by the flickering flame of the oil lamp while, to her left, Rick's silhouette stood out against the fading light of day. Through the dusky window she saw the sky had

turned into a fiery strip of orange. The floor was hard and cold.

"The sun will soon set," Maruk noted. "Where do we go now?"

"I don't know," Jason answered. He squeezed Maruk's hand, and somehow that gave them both a measure of hope. In the desolation of the Abandoned Corridors, hope was in short supply.

Rick walked up to one of the statues. He wiped away the cobwebs and soot that covered it. Rick soon realized that it depicted Major Arcana card number one: the Magician.

"Any ideas?" Jason asked.

"Maybe," his friend replied with his customary practicality. "If our guess was correct, then there are at least three rooms where we can start looking: the room of the Moon, Major Arcana card number eighteen; the room of the Star, Major Arcana card number seventeen; or the room of the Sun, number nineteen."

"Lover chasing lover," Maruk whispered.

"On the other hand," Rick added, "we could head in the opposite direction. There should be a room for card number six — the Room of the Lovers."

"Let's start there," Jason said decisively.

The three walked swiftly as the light of sunset cast

their long shadows onto the floor. Walking briskly helped fend off the sense of gloom that pervaded the Corridors.

Jason led the way, holding the lamp out ahead of him. The soot-covered mirrors did not provide much light, though he imagined in a different time the place would have been bright and cheerful. Now the niches looked like a series of dark, gaping mouths.

At each intersection, Rick checked the order of the Major Arcana in the dictionary so he could decide which direction to take. They made their way through the dank labyrinth without uttering a word. Somehow it did not seem appropriate to talk.

Suddenly, their shadows were swallowed up by absolute darkness, which obscured the ceiling and the walls. With each step they took, they stirred up little puffs of ash or scraps of papyrus from the ground, their feet crunching down on pieces of charred wood. Tears began to well in their irritated eyes.

"We must be getting close," Rick said. "The fire seems like it was even worse in here."

Hanging from the ceiling were cobwebs of black ash. Something blocked their way. Jason raised his oil lamp.

Maruk screamed, a piercing cry that echoed

through the desolate hallways. She turned and buried her face in Jason's shoulder.

Before them were two skeletons . . . locked in an embrace.

Strangely, Jason was not frightened. After all, he had been thinking about skeletons since he first stepped inside the Abandoned Corridors. Full of curiosity, he slowly moved the lamp over the two figures.

Some of their clothing was intact. The larger of the two skeletons, the man, had his back against the wall. In his arms he was cradling the smaller one, a woman, as if trying in vain to protect her. To Jason, despite the presence of death, there was something tender about the scene. He could imagine them still alive, surrounded by the smoke and flames. They must have stopped, surrendering to their fate, awaiting certain death in the comfort of each other's arms.

"Their souls grieve," murmured Maruk. "No one has prepared them for the journey to the Afterworld. They do not even have scarabs over their hearts, which should have accompanied them before Thoth and the great scale of Ma'at that weighs their actions, both good and bad."

Maruk kneeled down. She took off the amulet she

wore around her neck. She began to pray, caressing the stones on her necklace like a rosary.

Jason and Rick waited in respectful silence for Maruk to finish her prayer. Then they took out of their pockets the two scarab passes that they had received upon first entering the House of Life. They rested the scarabs gently on the two skeletons' skulls.

"May you find peace," Rick whispered.

Huddled together for comfort, the kids continued down the corridor until they came to a place where it opened into a large, square room. Inside there were two enormous statues, roughly fifteen feet in height. The statues were blackened with soot and ash.

"This is it," Rick said in a low voice.

Maruk let out a cry of relief. In the room was a large window that looked out over the courtyard of the House of Life.

The girl ran up to gaze at the orange-and-red sky. The red disk of the sun was poised above the horizon. She rested her hand on the windowsill, breathing in the fresh air.

"I feel like I've just come back to life," she said, without turning back to look at her friends. If she had done so, she would have noticed that their

clothes and faces were completely black, as if they had walked through a rainstorm of soot. All around them, in fact, were blackened debris and cobwebs, which hung from the two gigantic statues, billowing like fabric.

"Could the fire have started in here?" asked Jason. Pieces of charred papyrus crunched beneath his feet.

"From what we've seen, this room definitely got the worst of it," Rick replied.

"But did it start here?" Jason persisted. "If we can be sure of the fire's origin, then we'll know that we're in the right place."

Rick shrugged. He looked at the sun, which slowly began to fall behind the distant horizon. "I don't think we've got the luxury of time to be sure of anything," he concluded.

"Well, here's to second chances," Jason said.

"What do you mean?"

"Don't you realize?" Jason said. "We're attempting to do what Mammon tried — and failed at — once before."

Rick recalled the old man's story. "He said that he moved the mirrors . . . and that the sunbeams set fire to the papyruses." He spun around slowly, searching for a glint of reflected light. "Mirror, mirror on the wall," he murmured. "Where the heck are you hiding?"

He walked to the window and studied the horizon. He looked at the angle of the setting sun, then back at the room. His head, once again, was filled with mathematics. Trajectories and angles, distance and light. He pointed toward the statues. "If the mirrors capture the sunlight, they must face this window. The sun sets in the West, over there . . . so it rises from the East, down there. Which means that if there are mirrors in here, they have to be near those statues."

"Isis and Osiris," Maruk said softly.

"What?" Rick asked.

"Who," Maruk said with a smile. "The statues in this room are Isis and Osiris, the two lovers. After Osiris was killed by Seth, who chopped him up, Isis set out to search the Nile to gather the pieces of his body. After she found them all, she put the pieces back together, one by one, creating the world's first mummy. Isis used her magic arts to bring Osiris back to life." Maruk gave a bittersweet smile. "How strange. Maybe this is the secret of life that the two eternal lovers in the ballad were looking for: the magic of love, more powerful than death itself."

"Yes," Jason replied. "I think you're right. The two lovers should never have parted."

Jason moved closer to the statues, which were

obscured by a thick mantle of ash. Lifting the lamp over his head, he guessed that Isis must be the one on the right. High up, partially hidden in the darkness, he could just barely see the face of a woman. The hands of the statue had broken off, and her face, a black mask, gazed toward the window.

Osiris stood beside her, but his eyes looked only upon Isis. Jason rested the lamp on the ground. He began brushing away layers of ash, first at the feet, then the legs of the statue.

He bent over to pick up the lamp, and suddenly he saw it. On the head of Osiris, something sparkled, catching the sunlight.

"Rick!" he shouted. "The mirror! I found it! It's on the head of Osiris! Can you see it?!"

Rick dropped his bundle and pulled out a length of rope. "I *knew* this would come in handy," he exclaimed triumphantly. He quickly tied a slipknot and lassoed the rope around the statue's head.

"Excuse me, big guy," Rick said to Osiris. Then he began to climb up the statue.

"Be careful!" Maruk called.

"Are you kidding?" Rick answered back. "It will be a piece of caaaayyyy . . ."

A section of stone where Rick had planted his foot snapped off with a *crack* and he tumbled to the ground with a *thud*. Blushing with embarrassment, he picked himself up and started climbing once more.

In moments, Rick had reached Osiris's intertwined hands. He paused there, catching his breath. He found himself staring into the god's sculpted face, so that he and the statue were literally eye to eye. Then Rick tore off a strip of his linen shirt and began to wipe away the soot covering the statue.

"Hurry, Rick," Jason called out. He glanced out the window nervously. "The sun has almost set."

Rick rubbed the statue furiously, creating a dark cloud of ashes. Where was the mirror? Could they have been wrong? At last, he saw the faintest glimmer of light.

Yes! Hidden beneath that layer of black soot there really was a mirror! The same mirror that Mammon had told them about.

"There must be another one on top of Isis!" Jason shouted.

Rick slipped the rope off of Osiris and threw it down to the ground. Jason did not waste a second. He tossed the lasso end around Isis's head and used it to scramble onto the goddess's lap. On the crown circling her forehead, there was another mirror. Jason used his shirt to remove the soot left by the fire, polishing it vigorously.

"We did it!" he shouted, overjoyed.

But they had not yet completed the task. For at that moment, a final ray of sunlight danced across the sky. From the vast distance between sun and earth, a beam shined directly upon the head of Osiris.

For an instant, Rick was nearly blinded by the light. He shifted to the side, pulling the mirror back toward the god's shoulder.

Nothing happened.

Down below, Maruk instantly realized their mistake. "They aren't looking at each other!" she cried up at the boys. "The two lovers aren't looking at each other! The mirrors aren't reflecting off of each other!"

She was right. The sunbeam was reflecting off of Osiris, but it bounced onto the shoulder of Isis, where it died on the stone. "Her mirror won't budge," Jason cried. "I can't seem to move it!"

"We have to move the whole statue," Rick realized.

The two boys leaped down to the ground. Together, they threw their weight against the base of her throne. "You've got to move!" Jason shouted at the statue of Isis. "Look . . . your love . . . in the eyes!"

Maruk ran up beside Jason and Rick. She helped them push. Incredibly, slowly, the statue began to turn.

Isis moved along ancient tracks, cutting through the ashes that blocked the way. She circled around until she finally faced her beloved.

The moment their eyes met, the sun danced between their two crowns, reflecting off of the mirrors in a final farewell before nightfall.

Rick scurried up Osiris for a higher vantage point. He followed the beam as it shot back outside.

In the courtyard, on the other side of the wall, just outside the House of Life, a curtain of translucent light swayed in the air. Shimmering, golden, magical.

It revealed the entrance to the Room That Isn't There.

Nestor limped swiftly across the garden through the heavy rain. Deafening music blared out from Manfred's car. Nestor gave a start when he saw that the door to the caretaker's cottage was wide open, casting a warm yellow light through the trees.

Nestor cursed himself for leaving the house unlocked. "Stupid, stupid, stupid." He crouched down and circled the long way around the cottage.

"Where are you? Where are you?" he muttered to

himself, squinting in the darkness. A beacon from the lighthouse crossed the garden, and at last Nestor located his wheelbarrow. It was behind the trunk of a Japanese cherry tree, right where he'd left it.

He picked up the shovel that was inside the wheelbarrow. He felt it in his hands, checking its heft. He tried a couple of practice swings, bringing it down through the air in a wide, sweeping motion. It wasn't the perfect weapon, but it would do.

Nestor turned his eyes to the door of the cottage. Inside, he heard Manfred moving around. Slamming drawers. Throwing papers to the floor. Nestor gripped the shovel tightly. It would *have* to do.

Nestor burst into the house, taking Manfred by surprise. "Get out of here," the caretaker boomed, brandishing the shovel threateningly.

Manfred had been rummaging through the drawers of Nestor's writing desk. He looked startled, but not frightened. He subtly slipped something into his pocket.

"So you finally decided to stop cowering inside Argo Manor," Manfred said, facing the old man.

"Put back what you took," Nestor ordered.

Manfred gave him a lazy grin. "Or what?"

Nestor slammed the shovel against the wall. "Consider yourself warned," he whispered tightly.

Manfred raised his hands. "Hey, hey, take it easy. Don't get so bent out of shape, old man. It's not good for your heart."

Nestor felt a tingling in his hands. His forehead suddenly felt cold, clammy. He clutched the shovel tighter.

Manfred pointed at his own nose. "See what your little friend did to me? She broke my nose."

"You deserved it," Nestor replied. "You are lucky I haven't called the police."

"Be my guest," Manfred answered. "No phones are working in this storm."

"I said *get out*," Nestor repeated. "But first, return what you took."

Manfred slowly withdrew something from his pocket — a key. It looked ancient and heavy, similar to the four keys that opened the door in the stone room. "You mean this?" Manfred said, grinning slyly. "I don't know, I kind of like it. Finders keepers, you know what I mean? Besides," he added, "I figure that my boss will be real happy to have it — she might even give me a bonus!"

Nestor grasped the shovel and lunged at Manfred, narrowly missing him. Manfred swung around, keeping the desk between them.

"Careful, old man," he warned.

"OUT!" Nestor screamed.

The two began to circle each other slowly, moving around the desk like wary boxers in a ring. Though Nestor held the shovel, it was not at all clear that he had the advantage. Manfred was younger, faster, stronger.

Nestor swung the shovel again, smashing it against the desk. Manfred quickly reached for it, hoping to grab the shovel from Nestor. He missed — but the old man was already panting heavily.

"You are tired," Manfred said teasingly. "An old man like you really ought to be napping in your silk pajamas. This isn't a fight you can win."

"Put back that key," Nestor repeated.

Manfred laughed. "No."

Again Nestor swung the heavy shovel at Manfred, and again the younger man easily dodged the blow. As Manfred turned, he realized that they had changed positions. The front door was behind him. Nestor was on the other side of the desk.

Manfred held out a hand, trying to calm the angry old man. He slowly stepped backward. "Okay, nice and easy, you old coot. I'll give you the key. I didn't realize it meant so much to you."

He backed onto the wooden patio that surrounded the cottage. Keeping a wary eye on Nestor, Manfred slowly stepped down the two stairs that led to the garden. "Maybe I'll come back for another visit someday," Manfred said. "You know, just for kicks and giggles."

Nestor moved forward, shovel held high, ready to strike. "Place the key on the ground, get in your car, and never set foot on this property again."

Manfred bent down. He slowly lowered the hand that held the key, as though obeying Nestor's order.

"Say," Manfred suddenly exclaimed. "Where are your little buddies, anyway?" he asked. "Are they all hiding in the house? That's not very nice. Here you are all wet, while they wait inside, probably crying their little eyes out."

Nestor banged the shovel down against the wood of the patio. Manfred quickly leaped forward and grabbed it. He gave the shovel a fierce yank, forcing Nestor to the ground in the process.

"Nice try, old man," Manfred said mockingly. He pocketed the key.

Nestor got on his hands and knees. He tried to get up. But Manfred placed a boot on his back and pushed him to the ground again. "I didn't say you could get up."

Manfred half-turned, looking back at Argo Manor. "I wonder what you've got inside?" he said

aloud. "You don't mind if I take a look around, do you, old man?"

Fueled by fury, Nestor suddenly rolled to one side. He swept a leg under Manfred, knocking him to the ground.

Manfred sputtered, shocked, but quickly recovered. He leaped to his feet again. The shovel was in his hands.

"You shouldn't have done that, old man!" Manfred said. "You got my suit all dirty. Now you've made me mad."

He raised the shovel above his head.

And at that exact moment, the loud music coming from the car radio suddenly stopped.

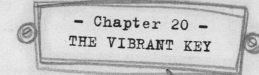

- Chapter 20 -
THE VIBRANT KEY

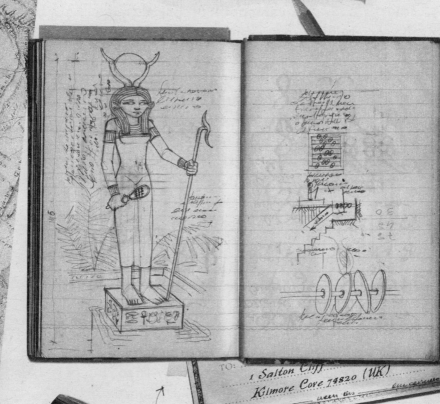

TO: 1 Salton Cliff
Kilmore Cove 74820 (UK)

I think Jason made this sketch of Isis. But
it might have been Ulysses Moore . . .

Rick led the charge. "The curtain of sunlight landed right outside," he called to Jason and Maruk. They followed as he led them through the courtyard to a square pool of placid water. In the center of it rose a statue of Hathor, the goddess of love and music.

"What did it look like?" Jason asked. Rick had been the only one of the three who was high enough to see outside the window. "Was it really like a curtain of light?"

"It was weird," Rick said. "Like, I don't know, waves of light floating in the air. It only lasted for a few seconds, but —" he pointed to the ground at the edge of the pool — "the wall of light was cast right . . . here!"

Rick dropped to his knees. With his bare hands, he scraped away the grass that grew to the edge of the stone rim of the pool, and then slipped his hand into the soft earth.

Maruk and Jason kneeled beside him to help. They pulled up tufts of grass, clearing away large clumps of earth. "I feel something!" Jason exclaimed.

Together, the three kids scraped and dug until they had uncovered a stone grate carved in the shape of a bell. It looked like a storm drain crossed over by eight bars of grooved stone.

Rick found a pebble and dropped it between two of the stone bars.

The pebble hit something metallic, and then knocked against a solid surface, possibly of stone, and bounced several times before settling.

"It sounds like there's a stairway down there," Jason said. Using the lamp, he tried to peer into the darkness below.

Maruk rose to her feet and looked around. They were in a small oasis where very few people ever went, probably because it was so close to the Abandoned Corridors.

"It really was right under everyone's nose," she said. "I can't imagine how many people have come right here, perhaps to sit and talk, without ever realizing that just under their feet . . ."

". . . was a secret room!" Rick exclaimed.

"Yes," Jason said, "the Room That Isn't There!"

"Let's try to pull it up," Rick suggested. "It looks like there's some kind of narrow passageway just below." He grabbed hold of one of the stone bars and pulled. Bizarrely, the grate did not move — it hummed!

"A chime?" Maruk said.

"Maybe it's stuck," Rick said. "Give me a hand, guys. Who knows how long its been since anyone opened it?"

The three kids pulled and pulled. But despite all their efforts, the grate would not move an inch.

Rick collapsed onto the grass, exhausted. "It's sealed off."

"There must be a way," Jason insisted. "There's always a way."

"What about that strange chime?" Maruk asked. "The song did mention a vibrant key."

Rick noticed that attached to the bottom of the grate's eight stone bars hung strange disks. He slipped his fingers between the bars and tapped on one of them. It chimed with the same sound that they had heard earlier. "Okay, let's think this through," he said.

"There's no lock. No nothing," Jason said. "Just those dangling cymbal-type thingies."

He lay down on his stomach to take a closer look. The cymbals were attached to the bars with bronze rings. Using a small stick, he could shift each cymbal from left to right to change its position. And when their position changed, so did the pitch of the chime.

"I'm stumped," Jason said, scratching his head.

Maruk began to say something, but then seemed to decide against it. She shook her head.

Rick took a turn studying the cymbals. They could

all be moved, although they seemed to be interconnected somehow. He counted them. There were sixteen cymbals in all, two for each horizontal bar.

"I don't understand any of this," he muttered. "I just don't understand what we're supposed to do."

"Could this be some kind of . . . sistrum?" Maruk asked, gathering up her courage. It was the first time she had seen Jason and Rick so thoroughly stumped by a riddle. Yet to her, it all seemed quite simple.

"What did you say, Maruk?" Jason asked.

"A sistrum," she said. "It's a popular musical instrument." Maruk pointed to the statue of Hathor, who stood in the middle of the pool. She was the goddess of music, and she held a sistrum in her hands.

"It's a percussion instrument," Maruk explained. "It can be tuned in different ways by positioning the cymbals, depending on which song you want to play."

"Do you know how to do it?" Jason asked.

Maruk shrugged. "It should not be difficult." She kneeled beside the grate. Before moving a cymbal, she looked up at her friends questioningly. "What song should I tune it for?"

"'The Ballad of Two Lovers!'" the two boys replied in unison.

Maruk carefully repositioned the cymbals along

the stone bars, sliding them this way and that, until she was satisfied with the sound of each individual tone.

"It's like tuning a piano or a guitar," Rick noted.

Maruk leaned back on her heels. "Finished," she announced.

"Yeah, but . . . nothing happened," Jason said.

"Maybe nothing is supposed to happen," Rick suggested. He grabbed hold of the grate and pulled it upward. Slowly, the grate gave way, almost imperceptibly. Jason helped him pull. It came free.

"Yes!" Jason cried.

Rick rested the grate on the grass beside the opening. Holding it upside down, he finally understood how the ingenious device worked. The cymbals were interconnected by a system of weights and cords. By placing them in the correct position, the system of cords freed a large, sturdy rope, which, in any other position, kept the grate sealed off from below, locking it into the wall.

"Now *that* is a clever lock," Rick remarked, fascinated.

Jason's thoughts were down below. He took the oil lamp and held it over the opening. His heart beat wildly.

"You see," he said to Maruk, his face beaming with pride and happiness. "I knew it existed. I knew it!"

"Yes," Maruk said to her friend. She placed a hand on his shoulder. "You were great. You had faith."

"And faith moves mountains!" Jason exalted. "Come on, let's check it out."

He stepped down onto the first of the series of narrow steps that were cut into the rock. They spiraled down into darkness below.

The three kids began their descent, with Jason leading the way.

The stairs were incredibly treacherous. Very narrow, very steep. Each step barely gave them enough room to gain a toehold, and each one was of a different height than the one before it, making each step they took seem like a small plunge into the void.

"The song never mentioned this," Rick grumbled. The air grew stuffy almost immediately. It smelled of mildew. The lamp tore through veils of spiderwebs that hung down like thick curtains.

"Guys," Jason called back to his friends. "Remind me next time not to take the lead. It's sort of gross down here."

"Oh?" Rick said.

"Yeah," Jason replied, coughing fitfully. "I think I just swallowed a spider!"

They could hear the sound of small creatures scurrying in the darkness, disturbed by their unexpected intrusion.

"I've hit the bottom," Jason announced. "This is it."

He raised his lamp, which shed a flickering golden light, and looked around in awe.

"Oh. My. God."

Julia had seen it all from the upstairs window. The moment that Nestor fell to the ground, she didn't hesitate. She flew down the stairs and out the glass doors of the portico. Without thinking she ran straight to Manfred's car. She had to find some kind of distraction, and she didn't have time to spare. So she did the only thing that came to her mind: She got into the car and turned off the blaring music. She paused for a moment, then turned off the headlights, too. For her plan to work, she would need the cover of darkness.

Julia crept back out and crouched behind the rear of the car, staying hidden from view.

"Aha," Manfred growled. "The little bird has flown from her cage."

"Run, Julia!" Nestor screamed as loudly as he could. "Run back inside the house! Hide! Lock the doors!"

"Oh be quiet," Manfred muttered. He dropped the shovel to the ground, then drove a steel-toed boot into Nestor's knee.

"Aaaaarrrghhh!" the old man screamed in agony.

A tremendous nervousness came over Julia. She turned to look at the house. The door to Argo Manor was just a few feet away. There was still time. She could run and hide. She could bolt the door like Nestor said.

But she stayed.

And she waited.

First, she heard Manfred's heavy footsteps approaching the car. Good. He was rushing, not being cautious. He was not the least bit afraid. Julia could use that to her advantage.

She crept around to the side of the car, closer, closer. At the last second, she dived out lengthwise and tripped Manfred, who fell facedown on the gravel with a heavy grunt. The wind was knocked out of him. All he could do, for the moment, at least, was lie there and try to catch his breath.

Manfred opened his eyes. He found himself staring at a puddle. And in the center of it, like a ship in the sea, was the key he had stolen from Nestor's desk. It had tumbled out of the pocket of his raincoat.

He reached out for it, but Julia beat him to it. She

snatched up the key. But Manfred lunged and tripped her. In a moment, he was back on his feet, standing between Julia and the door to Argo Manor.

The lighthouse beacon crawled across the grounds, giving the scene a dreamlike quality. But this was not a dream. It was a nightmare.

"Run, Julia!" Nestor shouted. "Run!"

Julia took off. She turned and headed toward Nestor's voice. She ran until she found herself staring straight down at the sea. She had run until there was nowhere else to run. She stood at the farthest edge of Salton Cliff, right where the stairs began their descent. At the place where just one day before, Jason had almost fallen to his death.

Julia turned. Manfred was a good thirty yards behind her, one arm clutching his ribs as he stumbled toward her. He looked exhausted. He slowed to a walk, then stopped, breathing heavily. He bent over with hands on his knees. Then he turned his head and looked back at Argo Manor, as if he was reconsidering.

Julia panicked. In her haste, she'd left the front door wide open. She couldn't let Manfred go inside Argo Manor! So she held the key above her head and waved it. "Come and get it," she yelled into the raging wind. "Come and try to take it away from me. I dare you!"

"No, Julia. It's not worth it," Nestor called. He was still on the ground, unable to walk. "Get away while you still can!"

But it was too late. Manfred began stalking toward Julia. "That's my key," he growled.

Julia smiled, betraying no fear. In truth, her heart was beating wildly. But she knew that in order to survive, she had to remain calm.

A clap of thunder shook the air.

"Give me that key and I won't hurt you," Manfred said. The threat of violence was thick on his tongue. Julia knew better than to trust him. He was now just three paces away from her.

"If you come one step closer," she warned, "I'll throw it into the sea."

"You wouldn't dare," Manfred said.

"Try me," Julia shot back, swinging the key between her fingertips.

"Hand it over," Manfred ordered.

"You know what I just realized?" Julia asked, smiling politely. "Seeing you right now, up close and personal like this?" She paused. "You look like a dumb cow. A big clod in a cheap raincoat."

Manfred lunged at her. But Julia was prepared.

She had expected this. In fact, she had hoped for it. She tossed the key into the air, hoping to distract him. Almost simultaneously, she dodged to the side and rolled into a somersault, barely escaping Manfred's outstretched arms.

The lighthouse beacon swung around, out into the ocean, back to the cliff, and again across the empty land around Argo Manor. By the time its turn was complete, Manfred had disappeared over the edge. He was gone.

Jason slowly swung the oil lamp around in front of him. It cast an arc of light into the Room That Isn't There. It was a deep, narrow room — a dark, ancient place carved by primitive tools.

Jason's flickering, unsteady light revealed rows of gold sarcophagi lined up against the side walls like guards standing at attention. Between the two rows of sarcophagi was a narrow stone pathway that led far back to a sort of altar filled with an odd assortment of treasures.

"Who were they?" Jason murmured, shining the pale light onto the faces carved into the gold surfaces of the sarcophagi. Their features were stern and incredibly ancient, almost alien in nature.

"The Founders," Maruk whispered. "Those who came from out of the sea to build the House of Life."

The Founders looked out before them, austere in their gold garments. Their arms were held straight down at their sides, and their feet rested atop large turtle shells.

The kids did not utter a word, taking in the majesty of their surroundings.

"Look!" Rick said a moment later, kneeling down on the ground. At the bottom of the stairs were three small objects covered with dust — tiny turtles carved in ivory.

Three turtles. The same creatures they had found on the archway over the door back in the grotto under Salton Cliff. Jason felt a shiver run down his spine. Somehow it was all connected. The Founders ... ancient Egypt ... and Argo Manor. What had they stumbled upon? What did it all mean? And why had Fate carried them here — to stand in a room that no one believed even existed?

When he took a step, Jason had the sensation of walking on a thin layer of snow. His foot sank a few inches into the sand, breaking through a crust before hitting the hard stone floor. "I want to check out that altar," he said.

Behind him, Maruk took a step forward. She had taken out her amulet and clutched it with both of her hands.

Rick followed close behind, looking around nervously. He felt uneasy down here, in this silent realm. He almost felt like he was disturbing the Founders' silent slumber, as if he had broken a moral code by entering this place. No good could come of it. Maybe Mammon was right. Maybe to want such a thing would only bring ruin to one's life.

The room echoed strangely with distant thuds and drops of water. It was hard to figure out the

source of the sounds. Rick thought he heard faint hissing noises, but his eyes could not confirm his worst fears. If there were snakes around, he didn't see any. Which, he admitted to himself, was better than the alternative.

"We're almost there," Jason whispered, pushing his way through spiderwebs and darkness. He was determined to find Ulysses Moore's map.

Suddenly, Jason stopped in his tracks.

"What's wrong, Maruk?" he asked.

"Nothing. Why do you ask?" the girl replied. She was standing immediately behind him.

"Then would you please take your arm off my shoulder?" Jason replied. "Your hand is kind of cold."

"Jason . . . ?"

"Yes, Maruk?"

"My hand isn't on your shoulder."

The light from the lamp wobbled unsteadily. "Well, if that isn't your hand," Jason said in a low voice, speaking very slowly, "then what have I got on my shoulder?"

"I can't see a thing," Maruk said. "Raise the lamp. Bring the light closer."

Behind them both, Rick whipped his head around. He stared back at the two rows of sarcophagi. For an instant — no, it was just his imagination — it seemed that something was moving near one of them. Creeping closer.

Jason lifted up the lamp until it cast light on his left shoulder.

"Oh no!" cried Maruk in a muffled whisper.

Jason slowly turned his head, a fraction of an inch at a time. The thing on his shoulder let out a hiss. It stared at him through cold yellow eyes.

A snake.

A big snake.

A very big scary snake.

Jason held back a scream. With a sudden gesture, he lashed at the reptile with his hand. The snake fell to the ground with a soft thud. It wriggled through the sand and slithered into the shadows.

"Whew," Jason sighed. "That was close." He raised the lamp to take a better look around.

It was not a good idea, at least as far as morale was concerned. Maruk screamed. The echoes bounced off the narrow walls, seeming to grow louder over time. Rick, a step or two behind her, stopped dead in his tracks. He did not scream. But then again, it's not easy to scream when you're frozen with fear.

There were snakes everywhere. Dozens of snakes. Hundreds of snakes. They dropped from the ceiling.

They slithered beneath the sand. They crawled out of clay pots, from behind ancient relics, even from out of the eyes of the sarcophagi. They were curling, entwining, coiling up — hissing and biting at one another, slipping in and out of the darkness.

"We've awoken them," Maruk whispered, terrified. "We've disturbed their rest."

"Rick?" Jason said in a hushed voice.

"Yes, Jason?"

"Any bright ideas?"

"Nope."

"Well, um, if you think of something, please let us know," Jason whispered. "Because we could sure use one of your patented Great Ideas right about now."

More snakes were raining down from above, hitting the ground with a *thup, thup, thup.*

"Rick?"

"Sssh! I'm thinking."

"Could you think a little faster?" Jason urged.

Maruk mumbled something to herself.

"Snakes are deaf," Rick remembered, trying to come up with any scientific fact that they might be able to use to their advantage. "What disturbs them are . . . vibrations," he said.

"Okaaay," Jason murmured. "I'll try not to vibrate."

"Fire," Maruk said. "Snakes fear fire. They hide

in the dark, in caves, behind walls, under rocks. They don't like the light."

Jason nodded thoughtfully. "Good," he said. "That's actually helpful. Thanks, Maruk."

Jason swung the lamp in a wide circle around their feet. It seemed to temporarily drive off the slithering, hissing mass.

"I have a suggestion," Rick offered. "What do you say we get the heck out of here, right now? I'm really not enjoying the company."

"Do you think they're poisonous?" Jason asked.

"I don't know," Rick said. "At this point, does it really matter?"

"We came to find a map," Jason suddenly declared. "I am not going to let some lousy snakes keep me from my destiny. We're so close. I can almost reach out and touch the altar."

"Jason, seriously, that's a bad idea," Rick said. "In a world of really bad ideas, that's one of the worst I've ever heard. We've got to back up slowly until we reach the stairs. Then we'll run for our lives."

"But Rick," Jason said calmly. "I'm only five feet from the altar."

"That's swell," Rick said. "But what if the snakes *are* poisonous? Is this where you want to die?"

"I am *sure* that some of them are poisonous," Maruk said. The fear dripped from her voice.

"Okay, guys, wish me luck," Jason said, ignoring their warnings.

He took a step toward the altar. He raised the lamp higher. Another step, then another. The altar was crowded with all sorts of objects, each of them covered with sand, dust, and cobwebs. There were jars full of exotic jewelry, tiny jeweled statuettes, golden hair combs, lavishly illustrated papyrus scrolls, and elaborately carved wooden cases. In short, treasures of every description.

And none of it meant a thing to Jason Covenant.

"Think, Jason. Think," he murmured to himself. Where among all this treasure could the map of Kilmore Cove be hidden?

Maruk let out a whimper. Jason took a step toward her, stomping on the ground. He swung the lamp near her feet. "Hold on, Maruk," he said. "We'll be out of here soon."

Jason recalled the papyrus that he found inside the niche. It read:

I have moved the map to a safe place:
The Room That Isn't There.

That meant the map could not have been here for a long time. A few years, perhaps. Maybe decades. But not nearly as long as this other stuff.

Jason reached out the palm of his hand. He gently touched the surface of the altar in a spot where there seemed to be fewer cobwebs, less dust.

A box, a comb, a tiny golden statue. What was he looking for, exactly?

"Jason!" Rick called. "We really, really need to leave now. I can feel snakes slithering across my feet."

"I'm hurrying as fast as I can," Jason whispered. His hand made its way over the altar top, brushing past some objects, looking beneath others. The map. The map of Kilmore Cove. Where was it hidden?

Jason searched his brain for some kind of clue. *Think, Jason. Think. Or . . . no. Better yet, don't think at all. Just follow your instinct.* He lowered the lamp to the floor.

"Jason? What are you doing up there?" Rick asked.

Jason Covenant closed his eyes. He imagined that he was walking into the Room That Isn't There. He had a map in his hand. He wanted to hide it in a safe place. It was an important map. A map that Oblivia Newton must not find. *Snakes,* he thought with a smile. That would help keep her away. For a while, at least.

His tongue felt swollen in his mouth. His head was pounding.

Jason took a deep breath. He turned his hands palm up. He reached beneath the altar. He felt around on the stone, then pressed gently.

Clack.

Something lightweight detached from the bottom of the altar. He held it in his hands. For a moment, all Jason could see was a grayish blur of snow, because he had shut his eyes so tightly.

When he pulled his hands back toward him, he realized that he was holding a flat wooden frame. It was about the size of a large photograph.

Jason turned slowly. Time stood still. He held the frame in the light.

It was a sepia print. It was . . . a map. Not a map,

THE FIRST AND ONLY
ACCURATE MAP OF THAT LAND
IN CORNWALL KNOWN AS
KILMORE COVE
LONDON

but *the* map! In a decorated border along the bottom were these words:

The first and only accurate map of that land
in Cornwall known as Kilmore Cove.

Jason stood staring at it, awestruck. Finally, he looked up at the others. "We found it! We've found the map of Kilmore Cove!"

That's when the flame from the oil lamp went out.

And that's when things got *really* interesting.

The three kids found themselves enveloped in darkness — a slithering, hissing, sliding, gliding, crawling darkness.

Jason held the map tightly to his chest. Maruk started to recite aloud the prayers that, until a moment before, she'd been whispering silently.

"Don't move," Rick said. "Stay absolutely calm."

"I'm too frightened to move," Maruk replied softly.

Rick rummaged around in his bundle of things. When he finally managed to light a match, his soot-darkened face appeared in a halo of trembling light. "We've got to light it again," he said. "Jason, hand the lamp to Maruk."

Jason reached down for the lamp, fumbling in the dark. The match burned down to Rick's fingers. He dropped it to the floor, which he could now see was completely covered with snakes. He lit another match.

"Just give me the matches," Jason said.

"No, pass the lamp to Maruk," Rick told Jason. "There's no time to argue about it."

Jason took a step toward Maruk and passed her the lamp.

"Got it!" Maruk exclaimed.

Rick's match went out. He pulled out a third one, preparing to strike it.

At that moment, a snake dropped down onto Maruk's head. She shrieked and flung her arms up in the air, desperate to get the creature away from her. The lamp flew out of her grasp and shattered against one of the sarcophagi.

Maruk turned and fled toward the door. She banged into Rick, knocking him against the wall.

"Run!" Jason shouted.

The three kids scrambled up the stairs with amazing swiftness. They emerged into the dusky twilight. Rick couldn't believe they'd escaped what had begun to feel like a slithering grave.

But there was no time to dwell on their lucky getaway. Because they found themselves standing face-to-face with an Egyptian boy, at least several years older than they were. He was sinewy, with dark eyes that gleamed dangerously, and he was dressed in rags. He held a long knife in his hand.

"Greetings," the young man said calmly. He gestured with his knife, ordering them to stand with their backs to the pool.

"Well, well, well," a woman's voice said. "Look what the cat dragged in."

It was Oblivia Newton. She headed straight to Jason, who tried to conceal the map behind his back.

"We have not been properly introduced," Oblivia said. She extended her hand. "You must be Jason."

"What do you want?" he snapped.

Oblivia leaned close to the boy. "You mean you really haven't figured that out yet?" She gestured to the young Egyptian man to take the map.

"No!" Jason shouted, holding it tightly.

The Egyptian struck Jason on the head with the blunt end of his knife, and he slumped to the ground, unconscious.

Rick stepped forward to join the fight, but a vicious kick to the stomach left him writhing on the grass.

Maruk kneeled down to comfort her friends. She looked up at Oblivia scornfully. "Thief!" she hissed.

The woman from Kilmore Cove took the frame out of the young man's hands. "Yes, thief," Oblivia sneered. "That's me. But who are you, with that absurd shaved head?"

Maruk lifted her chin proudly. "I am Maruk, daughter of the Great Master Scribe."

"Is that supposed to impress me?" Oblivia muttered in reply. With a snap, she broke the frame in half. Then she withdrew the map, unfolding it lengthwise. A satisfied smile crossed her face as her eyes greedily scanned it. "Ah yes," she purred. "I have searched for this for such a long time."

"Thief!" Maruk repeated.

"Drown her," Oblivia ordered the young Egyptian man, without taking her eyes off the map. "And lock the other two down there, in the pit. It must be near feeding time." With that, she rolled up the map and tucked it into her shirt.

The young Egyptian brandished his knife and stepped toward Maruk menacingly. Jason was lying on the ground, still unconscious. Rick struggled to his feet, placing himself between Maruk and her attacker.

"Stop!" a man's voice called out.

It was Mammon, the owner of the Shop of Long-Lost Maps. He hobbled out from the shadows. Each step looked like it caused him pain, though he did his best to mask it.

"We made a deal," he growled at Oblivia. "You get the map. I get the children."

Oblivia frowned, waving a perfectly manicured hand. "Whatever," she said. "I was just trying to have a little ... fun." She nodded her head to Mammon. "And now, I shall leave this place and return to my home."

"That is wonderful news! Truly wonderful!" Mammon answered, clapping his hands. His face was dark with anger. "Go," he told Oblivia, "and never, ever let me see you again. Do you understand me?"

Oblivia blanched. Her eyes moved to Rick, Jason, and Maruk. "Ta-ta," she said.

The old man glared at his assistant. "How dare you even think of carrying out an order like that? These are children!"

Oblivia laughed hatefully. "Pests is more like it," she said. "Pests that are best exterminated."

"Go!" Mammon commanded her. "I gave you my word — you may take the map. But by the gods above and the gods below, I will snap your neck if you stay here another instant!'

Oblivia took a half step back. Her eyes went to Mammon's assistant. "I will need a guide," she said.

The old man nodded. "Go," he ordered. He dismissed them both with a wave of his hand. The two melted away into the hazy dusk.

Left alone with the three explorers, Mammon stretched out his swollen foot to nudge Jason, who was still sprawled on the ground. "Wake up, Dagger Tongue." He looked at Rick. "Heart of Stone," he said. "How are you feeling, my friend?"

Rick coughed a few times. He spat. Blood came from his mouth. He forced himself to stand erect.

The old man watched him. "Probably a cracked rib or two," he concluded.

"Why?" Rick asked. "I don't understand. Why did you help her?"

Mammon shrugged. "Business," he said. "She paid me to find the map."

"And you used us to do it," Rick said.

"I could see that you were bright and determined," the shop owner replied.

Jason groaned softly. Maruk filled her hands with water from the pool and sprinkled it on Jason's face. Jason suddenly sat up. He winced and felt the side of his head. Then he looked around, still groggy. His eyes widened in surprise when he saw Mammon. "Where did the others go?" he asked.

"They left," Maruk said. "You are safe now."

"And the map?" Jason asked.

Maruk bit her lip. Rick looked down at the ground. "Gone," he finally answered.

Jason's head seemed to clear. He pointed at Mammon. "What are you doing here?" he asked.

The old man raised both hands. "Business," he replied. "Money talks."

"How could you?" Jason said.

"Like I said before, it's business," Mammon explained. "It's not personal." He smiled at the kids, then slapped the back of his hand into the palm of the other. "I like you very much. The trouble is, I like money even better."

Jason just shook his head sadly. "You were ruined in that fire," he muttered.

The old man sighed. "Perhaps, yes, that's true. I am not the man I once was."

He walked up to the grate that had hidden the staircase. It was still lying on the grass. "I have to admit it," he said, shaking his head. "You kids have accomplished something that I never would have imagined possible. I spent years looking for the Room That Isn't There, and you found it in a single afternoon."

Once she was outside the House of Life and in the city, Oblivia Newton dismissed her guide. She strode off at a brisk pace, taking great care to make sure that she was not followed, for she knew that Mammon's assistant was a child of the streets and a thief. After she was convinced that the young man was really gone, she retraced her steps, heading into a different section of the city.

As a final precaution, Oblivia paused at the corner opposite the house she wished to enter. She waited and watched. It was important that she move unseen. Still, she was bursting with eagerness. Oblivia could not wait to return to Kilmore Cove, where she could examine the map in solitude, safe from prying eyes.

Finally, after what seemed an intolerable wait, Oblivia crossed the street. She walked directly to a modest building. There appeared to be nothing special about it. But appearances can deceive. Oblivia look around one last time. The street was quiet. No one was watching. She slipped through the entrance.

There was no one inside. The building was empty, abandoned.

The wooden door was in the basement, hidden behind old furniture and strips of papyrus reed. Ulysses Moore had once tried to seal off this door. He had failed.

"Now I will find every last door," Oblivia said to herself. She clutched the map in cold triumph. She kicked aside a table and stood before the door.

She took out the key with the cat-shaped handle. But — strange — she did not have to use it. The door was unlocked.

"Learn something new every day," she mused, returning the key to her pocket. "Now I know that the key is needed only from the other side."

It was an interesting detail, but unsettling. It could be dangerous — very, very dangerous. What would happen if someone else found the door? Someone from this place? From this . . . time?

She would worry about it later. Oblivia pushed open the wooden door and crossed over the threshold. In moments, she was inside the home of Cleopatra Biggles. Oblivia checked her watch. It was working again.

The cats scampered around, hissing and mewling, agitated by her sudden arrival. Oblivia walked into the living room. "Manfred?" she called out.

Cleopatra Biggles was still asleep on the sofa, her mouth open wide. A cat was curled in the crook of her arm.

Oblivia glanced out the window. The rain had died down. The sky was dark. It was still night.

"Manfred?!" she called out impatiently.

Oblivia finally noticed that the car was gone. "You thick-headed mule," she moaned. "Where have you gone off to now?"

Oblivia took out the map. She carefully unrolled it on the dining room table. And then a slow smile spread across her face. Who cared if Manfred was gone? What did it matter about a car? She would buy more cars, as many as she wanted. She would hire another driver, or dozens of drivers. Nothing could stand in her way now. Nothing.

Oblivia paused in the sitting room. She picked up her fur coat from the floor. Then she left the house, resolved to make the long walk home. She didn't mind. Nothing could bother her now. She wrapped her fur around her and smiled. Life couldn't be better.

Oblivia Newton was in a wonderful mood.

- Chapter 23 -
BACK AT HOME

Argo Manor

Mammon left Rick, Jason, and Maruk alone in the courtyard. *He is truly a strange old man,* Rick thought.

Tired, depressed, and filled with a sense of failure, the three kids made their way back to the House of Visitors. Rick and Jason cast a final glance at the walls of the House of Life. Then they all headed down into the underground storeroom.

They entered the room where their journey had begun. They had come full circle to the room where they first met Maruk. The boys moved the board aside, revealing the hole in the brick wall.

There was a long silence. No one said a word. No one knew how to say good-bye.

"I think," Maruk finally said, "that now our lives must take different paths."

Rick looked down at the ground shyly. He nodded.

Jason rubbed his eyes, still feeling the effects of that blow to the head. He smiled sadly at Maruk.

The Egyptian girl slipped the amulet from around her neck. She placed it in Jason's hand. "It would mean a lot to me if you would take this with you," she said. "It would be like bringing a piece of me . . . into your world."

Jason was reluctant to accept the gift. "Maruk,

no," he said. "This amulet is important to you. I've watched you with it, holding it close to your heart."

Maruk held a finger to her lips. "It is a gift. The eye of Horus will look over you and protect you from misfortune, just as it protected me."

Rick set his bundle down on the ground. "One gift deserves another." He pulled out the last of the matches. "It's kind of lame, I know," he said. "But they are for you to remember us by and, um, maybe to give you a little light in times of darkness."

Maruk graciously accepted the matches.

The three friends stood awkwardly in silence, thinking back over everything that had happened to them on this incredible day.

"Will we meet again?" asked Maruk.

"I hope so," Jason replied.

They all hugged.

"I am sorry about the map," Maruk said sadly.

"We'll find a way to get it back," Jason quickly replied.

Rick shot him a wary look, then nodded in agreement.

There was nothing left to say.

"Go on, then!" Maruk said, waving them off with her hands. "Hurry before I try to follow you through that door!"

Rick and Jason climbed through the wall. They did their best to seal off the hole behind them. They could hear Maruk doing the same thing on the other side. When they'd finished, Jason rapped one last time on the bricks to say good-bye.

One knock. Two knocks. One knock. Then two more in quick succession. It was a fitting way to say good-bye.

The boys walked down the stairs. They turned the corner and reached the door.

"Here we are," Rick said.

Jason stared at the door. "You know what really makes me angry?" he said.

"What?"

"After all this trouble, we don't even know why that map is so important! Big deal, so Kilmore Cove was written on it! But who knows what any of it means?! Why did Ulysses Moore hide it in Egypt in the first place?"

Rick nodded. "Hopefully we'll find the answers one day."

They would seek the answers on another day. But for today, there was only the door that waited before them. All they had to do was walk through it.

Soon everything would be the same again. Yet the boys were changed forever.

Jason took a deep breath. "Ready?"

Rick nodded. "As I'll ever be."

Together, they crossed the threshold.

Badly hurt, Nestor hobbled toward Julia, using a gardening rake as a crutch. He found her near the cliff. She was on her hands and knees, searching through the grass.

She looked up at him. "I can't find it," she told Nestor. "The key. It should be here, but . . ."

Nestor placed a hand on her shoulder. "*Shhh*," he said. "Let's go inside."

Julia looked away, out over the cliff. Her lips trembled. She blinked away some tears. "But your key," she said, combing her fingers through the grass again.

"Come," Nestor said. "It is late and dark. We can look for the key tomorrow."

He hobbled forward another step, wincing. He held out a hand for her.

"Are you hurt?" she asked him.

Nestor shook his head. "Not too badly," he said. "But it has been a long, hard night. And you?"

"I'm a little scared," Julia admitted. "Do you think he's . . . dead?" She asked in a hushed voice. Again, she looked out at the sea.

Nestor frowned. He did not answer.

"Do you think it was my fault?" she asked.

"No, child," Nestor said kindly. "You are innocent. That man brought it upon himself."

He moved off in the direction of Manfred's car.

"Nestor?" Julia called. He was always walking away without a word of explanation. She trailed after him.

Nestor climbed into the car, behind the steering wheel. He turned on the ignition.

"What are you doing?" asked Julia.

"I'm getting this out of the way. I'll be back in a moment, Julia. Please wait inside." He closed the door and slowly inched the car forward using his uninjured leg. He did not turn on the lights.

Once inside, Julia became aware of how wet she was from the rain, and how cold. She walked into the stone room. The door was still closed. Julia grabbed a blanket and curled up on the sofa.

When she opened her eyes again, Nestor was beside her.

He smiled. "Pleasant dreams?" he asked.

Julia blinked. She wanted to speak with the old man. Ask him a hundred more questions. But her eyes wouldn't stay open. She was so tired, so very tired.

Her eyes opened. "We aren't going to tell, are we?" she whispered.

"It will be our secret," Nestor answered.

Her eyes closed. She felt her muscles relax, and her bones seemed to melt into the sofa. So tired, so very tired. "Jason and Rick," she murmured, half asleep. "They'll come home, won't they?"

Nestor brushed her hair back with his hand. He pulled the blanket around her. "*Shhh*," he said soothingly. "Sleep now, dear child. Yes, they will come home."

Julia smiled at the thought. She felt light as a feather, drifting, then floating on a breeze. A great happiness filled her spirit. The sky was clear. The sun was shining. And she was flying, flying high above the sea.

Another moment passed in her dreamscape. She felt a cold draft. The door . . . had opened. "We're home!" her brother cried out.

"Julia! Nestor! We're home!"

She heard Rick's voice, and Nestor's, and the sound of laughter.

The blankets were so warm and soft. And she felt tired, so very tired. Her eyes refused to open. But she understood that, outside, the storm was finally over.

When dawn came, the storm that had raged down upon Kilmore Cove faded away. The clouds drifted off, letting the first rays of sunlight shine through. Seagulls swooped down over the waves, hungry for fish. The sea swelled with rolling waves.

The storm had driven thick bunches of seaweed, driftwood, and old pieces of fishing nets up onto the beach. There was a tree trunk a few yards long . . . an old, torn sail . . . and other wreckage from ships battered and lost at sea.

And there was a man.

He was stretched out facedown in the sand. Motionless. He wore dark clothes and a raincoat. He was missing a shoe. The water lapped at his legs.

At last, the man coughed. He spat seawater from his mouth. His lips were dry and brittle. His body ached.

The man sat up. He moved one leg, then the other. He felt his arms and ribs. Nothing seemed to be broken.

He felt his nose. Well, almost nothing.

His right hand was bloody. It throbbed. Something was clutched inside of it, as if his fingers had a life of their own. He used his left hand to pry it open.

He smiled. Oblivia would be pleased. He had ideas. He could do stuff. He didn't always have to be told.

Manfred held a key in his hand.

A key with a lion-shaped handle.

Hi all,

Things just keep getting stranger and stranger here in Cornwall. When I woke up this morning, an envelope had been shoved under my door. I'd hoped that it was those letters from readers that you'd promised to forward to me. I can't wait to hear what they have to say about Ulysses Moore, and where I should be looking for him.

But instead it was a single page, torn from what looked like <u>more</u> of Ulysses's journals. How many can there be? The only text I can decipher on that page says something like "house of mirrors." The last time I found something like this, it led to a whole new manuscript. Maybe someone here in Zennor can point me in the right direction. . . .

More soon! Please send along readers' letters and advice whenever you can. I'm determined to get to the bottom of this mystery.

MM